T0196815

Essence of Jasmine

A. L. LaFleur

authorHOUSE®

AuthorHouse™
1663 Liberty Drive
Bloomington, IN 47403
www.authorhouse.com
Phone: 1 (800) 839-8640

S. Hill, editor

Published by AuthorHouse   09/30/2015

ISBN: 978-1-5049-3263-9 (sc)
ISBN: 978-1-5049-3262-2 (e)

Library of Congress Control Number: 2015913844

Print information available on the last page.

Prologue

After leaving Iguana Lounge following the intense conversation with Jasmine, Morgan had to sit in her Jaguar a moment and collect her thoughts. The idea of being with the man who gave her such intense pleasure had her mind reeling, and she couldn't stop herself from snatching up her cell phone and calling him. To her delight, he picked up before the first ring was complete. Immediately, he asked, "Has Jasmine been to see you?"

The expectancy in his voice caused her heart to jump, and she answered him in a voice that was nearly trembling. "She has. Can we talk?"

Before the words had quite left her mouth, he interjected, "I am right by you at the Colcord. Come to me." Jotting down the room number, she quickly exited the parking lot and made her way to him: the man who consumed her every waking thought and made her blood sizzle.

When she arrived in front of his door, her legs already felt like wet noodles from the anticipation and the desire she felt for him. Before she was able to knock, the door swung open and John picked her up, pulling her into his arms in a desperate embrace that had both of them breathing heavily.

Wrapping her legs around him, she could already feel his erection where her body came up against his, pushing into her sensitive skin, and trying to make its way inside her. She began to rub against him, pelvis on pelvis, as they grinded against each other. Morgan could hear a hiss as his breath rushed out swiftly, and he seemed to have difficulty maintaining his self-control; it was apparently all he could do to resist taking her right there in the hallway.

Opening his eyes to the very public surroundings where they so intimately embraced was likely all that kept John's willpower intact, and he immediately took a step backwards, before pulling her into the room and slamming the door.

Once inside, he held back no longer. It seemed he was barely able to push her panties aside in order to be inside her, his hands trembled so much. But after getting his pants just out of the way, he entered her. Against the door to his room, they frantically thrust into each other with their tongues and their bodies. So hungry for each other, they lasted only short moments before they both climaxed together.

Morgan's legs were so weak from the effort and the desire that she was thankful when he carried her to the bed. He lay down on her while still inside her, touching her face softly and gently, with a love that was palpable. Breathless, they stared into each other's eyes.

"My love, I am afraid I cannot get enough of you," he exclaimed, as he continued his loving caresses.

She returned the sentiment by stroking his face and pulling his face toward her mouth. "I have missed you terribly," she said after a breathy kiss that prompted him to move inside her again, sending waves of pleasure through both of them. "I don't know what I did with myself before you. I...I don't know what you have done to me John, but I have fallen in love with you."

She made her statement and then awaited the expected withdrawal, both physically and emotionally. The last lover she had made the admission to shut her down for it, leaving her feeling fragile and empty. She hadn't realized how vulnerable she felt about saying it until that moment; she held her breath, preparing for John to reject her.

As John hovered over Morgan, lovingly gazing down at her, it seemed to her that his heart was full to bursting when she made the statement. He had used the L word with her on many occasions, and she had steadfastly avoided using it. Suddenly, noting his reaction, Morgan wondered if he sensed the significance of her expressing it for the first time; for her, it was a gift she gave him. Feeling the old pain creep in, she wondered if she could keep the vulnerability at bay long enough to treasure the moment.

Her thoughts were interrupted when he kissed her mouth, dipping his tongue in while inhaling her essence. She gave back equally, moving to envelope him as she held him close, wanting him to be as deep inside her as possible.

Soon, however, he withdrew slightly, pushing himself up with his arms, though staying connected to her. Her momentary disappointment at his withdrawal was palpable, and he soon returned to briefly capture her mouth again before raising himself to hover over her.

"I need to be inside of you more, my love." As he settled on his knees, poised above her, he pulled her to him and directed her, moving her feet to rest on his shoulders. Once he had her in the desired position, he thrust himself into her passionately, as if seeking to embed himself in her forever.

"Oh, John!" Her cry echoed within the confines of the room. As if he was unable to control himself, he began pistoning into her, going deeper with each stroke. As the pressure built higher and higher, her head tossed from side to side until it was almost too much. John watched her face as she moaned, but could contain himself no longer. His orgasm had him crying out her name and then collapsing next to her.

Unfinished but so close, Morgan grinded her bottom into his lap, prompting him to look at her.

Instantly, she saw that he realized that he had finished before she was able to orgasm, and he moved to correct it.

Withdrawing from Morgan elicited a throaty moan from her, and he quickly replaced his phallus with his mouth, causing her hips to lift and another moan to escape her lips. As she fisted her hands in his hair and rode his tongue, the waves of pleasure grew higher and higher. Somewhere in the recesses of her mind, the thought occurred to her that he was savoring the taste of her as he lapped up her flavor. The pulses of delicious sensations that he doled out drove her to the edge. All she could do was curl her fingers tighter in his hair, holding on for dear life, until finally, she flew apart in his mouth.

Working to regulate her breathing, she lay back with glazed eyes in a state of bliss, still gripping his hair. As she settled into the bed, he rested his head on her thigh with her other leg draped over him while he studied her face.

They lay in a tangled heap like this for a while until she stirred and motioned for him to take his place next to her. He did as requested, pulling her close, until they fell asleep wrapped in each other's arms.

Chapter One

As Jasmine left Iguana Lounge, she had to sit in her Range Rover and force herself to breathe slowly. She had just essentially given another woman permission to take her husband from her, and it was with shaking hands that she managed to start the ignition. As much as she knew John no longer loved her and was constantly angry with her over her affair with his brother, the thought of being alone in a country that was not her own, with no family other than her young daughters, terrified her.

What to do now, she asked herself, and her thoughts turned to Patrick. She loved him so much that her heart ached. After the brief time they had been together, being without him reminded her of the words of a song she had recently heard: she felt like she'd been locked out of heaven.

Emerging from her reverie, she knew she had a decision to make: call Patrick, or wait a few days until he returned from Ireland. She calculated that it was just after ten at night there. He would likely be in the process of retiring for the evening.

She picked up her cell and started to dial. Halfway through his number, she stopped herself. *What if he doesn't want me?* she worried. He had professed his love for her often during their lovemaking, but what if it was just something he said in the throes of passion?

She thought back to the last time she had seen him. It was just last week, after he had toured the house across from hers. He had noticed her waving to him and had made a very quick exit, looking terrified.

Jasmine hugged herself and buried her face in her hands, conflicted. Eventually, she decided that she would rather wait until he returned. She made her way home, intent on spending time with her children and keeping her mind off of her beloved.

****

Patrick tossed and turned. He had been unable to sleep more than a few hours at a time since seeing his lover after all those months. Every time he closed his eyes, he saw her face. When he lay alone in bed at night and the pillow brushed against his lips, he couldn't help but taste her in his mouth. The pillow cover still held her scent, and sleeping with it was almost too much for him to bear.

Moaning and fatigued from his persistent insomnia, Patrick threw the covers off and went to his easel. Since losing Jasmine, the only thing that took his mind off of his obsession was painting. He shook his head at the irony, considering that she was his muse. In the months since she had gone away, he had amassed a large collection of her portraits. He instructed the servants to destroy them as soon as he completed them, and he imagined Jasmine's eyes staring at him as the flames consumed her flawless beauty.

Patrick shook his head to clear it. He had tried endlessly to forget about his brother's wife, but without success. Unfortunately, he suspected that her youngest child belonged to him, and he couldn't help but fantasize about a life where he could have the woman of his dreams anytime, growing old together with their beautiful daughter by their side. He had even begun painting Callista into the portrait with her mother. He hadn't been able to bring himself to destroy the ones with the girl, however, and his closet was beginning to overflow with them.

Studying his current painting brought his brooding to an abrupt halt. There beside Jasmine and his daughter- as he'd begun to think of her- was himself gazing upon them. The portrait was so lifelike that it amped up his obsession to a whole new level. He brought his hand to the canvas and caressed his beloved's face, stroking the lips with the pad of his thumb. He placed his other hand over his chest, hoping to soothe the ache there.

As he fondled and studied the portrait, he decided he could no longer stifle the feelings he had for Jasmine. Making up his mind, he began packing and planning an impromptu return to the States.

****

Shannon Kelly was a master of his trade, and he greatly enjoyed his work. Creating the brews that folks enjoyed in his pub had made him something of a local legend. He was also an excellent listener, and townspeople came as often for "therapy" as they did for his specialty brews. Most who had lived in their village for any length of time held him in high esteem and would go out of their way to see him and have one of his signature draft beers.

Unfortunately, not everyone thought so highly of him. As he wiped down the bar, he reflected that it was too bad his wife Siobhan didn't appreciate his attributes. Drawn to her years ago for her vibrant personality and beauty, Shannon had started courting her as soon as she reached the proper age. She had professed her love quite early in their courtship, making him believe that they were destined to be one of the great couples.

Looking back, he could see how foolish he had been. In truth, from the beginning, he'd had misgivings. His mother had never liked her; she said that his wife was a wolf in sheep's clothing. His best friend claimed that she'd lain with him before her and Shannon's wedding night. The shiner and broken nose he'd given for that one, though usually forgiven between the two, turned out to be a death blow to their friendship; that was the last time he'd seen Adam. Funny, he thought, that he was just now examining that night and considering the probability that Adam had been speaking the truth.

Shaking his head, he polished the brass at the end of the bar and continued to contemplate the choices he'd made that had brought him to the present, with the stark loneliness and the aching in his chest. His reverie was interrupted by a patron entering his establishment. Looking up, he immediately recognized Patrick from the Kennedy's.

As closing time was not far off, Shannon was inclined to turn him away; however, the saddened look on the man's face gave him pause. Instead he asked, "What'll it be, me old friend?"

Patrick shook the rain from his slicker before setting it on a barstool, claiming the adjacent one for himself. "Whiskey will do 'er," he announced, as he ran his fingers through his hair.

Whiskey was often requested by those drowning their sorrows, Shannon knew, so he poured a glass for both of them and stood across the bar from Patrick. "Cheers, lad," he saluted. They touched their cups and then drank, after which Shannon locked the door and turned the sign around to announce that his establishment was closed.

After six shots, Patrick began opening up about his brother's wife. Occasionally, Shannon chimed in, feeling the same acute sense of loneliness as his comrade. Eventually, he told Patrick his tale of how his wife had left him, stating that she had never wanted a family; she had merely wanted to be a barkeep's wife. Siobhan had then revealed the six secret abortions that she'd had. Some were too far along for Shannon to consider it anything but murder.

As Shannon became worked up by the whiskey and the unhealed hurt, he demanded, "I helped to create the babe! It was part of me also! Why does she get to be the only one to choose? I know, mate, it's her body, but it's me wee little one. Where are *my* rights as a parent?" As he expressed his anger and frustration at the injustice, he pounded his fist, causing the glasses on the bar to jump.

There was an acute sense of commonality between the old friends; this became more evident as Patrick opened up further about his brother's wife. Not that Jasmine had ever tried to keep Callie away from him, Patrick explained. But as he was not married to the girl's mother, he truly had no rights to the child. Eventually, Patrick– owing to the similarities in their shared circumstances and needing some company– invited Shannon to the States with him.

Twelve hours later, they were in flight together and heading toward Middle America.

****

After arriving at home, Jasmine went straight to the nursery. Spending time surrounded by reminders of her marriage was too much for her to take in her present state of mind, so she chose to occupy herself with her precious children, avoiding the rest of the house. She decided she had made the right decision when Callie jumped from her mother-in-law's arms into hers and expressed unabashed enthusiasm at seeing her.

It was no surprise that John's mother took the opportunity to sniff in her direction and ask accusingly, in her thick accent, "Where has me son gone to? Have ye sent him away again?"

Jasmine had always ignored her biting comments easily, but in light of her current precarious situation, she cringed internally and announced, "He will return soon, Brunne. You may go do whatever it is that you do with yourself now. I will care for the children myself." Seeing her blatant dismissal, her mother-in-law gave a disdainful sniff and left the room with her head held high.

Jasmine waited until the door closed behind her mother-in-law before playing the familiar game with her child. Squealing in delight, Callie grabbed her mother's face and laughed contentedly as she was tickled relentlessly. Looking at her napping four-year-old, Jasmine shushed her toddler, not wanting her to awaken her older sister.

Looking over, Callie imitated her mom and said, "No wake Deeda?"

Jasmine kissed her sweet child's forehead and confirmed, "That's right my little cherub, don't awaken Deirdre." Almost as if she had been summoned, Deirdre began to stir. Upon seeing her mother in the nursery, she jumped out of bed and placed herself in her mother's lap, all but pushing Callie out of the way.

Jasmine hugged both girls to her breast and rocked them gently in her lap, singing a lullaby to them. When she finished, Deirdre turned to her and asked, "Mama, when will Dadda be home?"

Jasmine had always known that, while Callie clung to her, Deirdre was closer to her father; but given the current situation, she felt hurt by her daughter's standoffishness. Swallowing back tears, Jasmine told her firstborn, "Daddy had to go away on business tonight, Love, but if you want we can call him first thing in the morning." Not satisfied, Deirdre pouted and crossed her arms over her chest.

"You are so like your father, my strong little one," she said, as she tucked the girl's hair behind her ear. The strands did not stay put for long however, because Deirdre promptly removed them and made a show of messing up her hair as she displaced it. Surprised that she remained on her lap, Jasmine chided her for her behavior. "Don't be so contrary, little one. Your father will return, and when he does he will be unhappy that you have been so difficult." This had the child straightening her hair, but continuing to pout. Callie observed her sister quietly while snuggling further into her mother's shoulder.

"That is better, my little one," she told Deirdre, and then feigning excitement she didn't feel, added, "I know! Why don't we go downstairs and see what kind of ice cream we have."

Callie immediately jumped off of her lap while Deirdre merely stood up and slowly walked toward the door. "I'd rather my Dadda were here, but ice cream would be nice," she announced. Jasmine always had difficulty with her oldest child, but was resigned to the fact that she was closer to her father.

"Come on then, maybe when Dadda gets home you can talk him into adding a swimming pool this summer," Jasmine suggested.

Deirdre immediately perked up and yelled, "I will! We need a pool!"

As they walked toward the kitchen, it was to a chorus of, "We get a pool...we get a pool!" Jasmine sighed, and decided it would probably be a long evening, figuring that John would likely be occupied with his lover all night.

Chapter Two

Rousing in her lover's arms, Morgan shifted to plant a kiss on John's mouth. He instantly awakened and returned the affection, touching her face and pulling her closer to him. Following the gentle kiss, he announced, "Its six o'clock in the morning, *mo ghra*. What do you have planned for yourself today?"

She sat up and stretched, contemplating her last several unproductive days. With a grimace, she recalled that there was quite a bit of unpleasant work to be done. "Let's see. I need to return some phone calls for work, get a door for my house, and talk to a detective or two." She rushed through the last part, hurrying on with, "Oh, and grocery shopping. I probably need to do some of that also."

Not wishing to explain the events of the last several days, Morgan started to move away to go to the bathroom, but was stopped when his arm snaked around her waist, pulling her against him in one smooth motion.

"What was that, my sweet? A new door and detectives? Did someone break into your house?" She pushed at his chest in an attempt to get away. Her efforts were in vain, however, due to his incredible strength. He held her wrists easily, watching her futile struggle with a mischievous grin.

Seeing that she was getting nowhere, she settled into him and with a sigh admitted, "I might have kind of shot a man yesterday."

Gripping her wrists overly tight, he pulled her closer, causing her to wince. She tried to hide her face in his chest, but with one hand under her chin he forced her to look at him. With the other hand, he held her wrists while wrapping his legs around her, effectively trapping her against his body.

"I know you are not thinking of keeping this from me, little doll. I will not stop until I know of what has taken place, and when my mind is made up I see that my will is carried out. Stop trying to avoid telling me so that I can save my strength for the fun things I want to do to you." He said the last while grinding his shaft into her thigh, and his relentless smile continued.

She sensed his implacable resolve, and resigned herself to telling him of her recent ordeals. "I...I...a man was stalking me," she started slowly, unsure of where to begin. John listened patiently, giving her time to collect her thoughts. She watched his face, expecting that he might have an explosive reaction when he heard the gory details of her story.

"A few weeks ago, he called my boss and was saying I'm evil and need to be killed...and he said the same for my kids." She had to swallow tears as the memory of him threatening her children lingered. "He became escalated last week. He sent me thousands of emails with horrible stuff, including pictures. He took photos of my billboards and did things with them; he posed them as though they were me after being cut up, and added blood to them. The things he said were really derogatory, calling me names like cunt and whore in his messages and emails." The calm was fading from John's face, replaced by an expression of anger.

She took a deep breath and then continued. "Well, at first when he called we were a little worried, and my boss called the police. I added security cameras to my house and bought some guns." As she explained the measures she had taken, John worked to keep his fury in check.

"I felt safe, at least at home. But then my ex-husband showed up out of the blue. We hadn't seen him since he left, so it was a bit of a shocker when he came to the house. As it turns out, he was having me watched and followed. I didn't know at first what he was doing." She paused for a moment to collect her thoughts and decide where to go next with the story. "But after Monday night I found out, and it was not pretty." She braced herself, wondering if John would freak out when she told him of the events of that night. It seemed so distant, but was in fact only two nights ago.

"I woke up around four in the morning because I heard scratching at my window. I looked at the backyard surveillance camera, and Steve was there by my bedroom window; that's my ex-husband. So I called 911. I had just yelled at Steve last week to stay away from me, so I damn sure didn't want him creeping around in my backyard at four in the morning." She paused for a moment, curious about his reaction. When his face remained impassive, she continued.

"After I got off the phone with the police I looked at the video again and saw someone else walking by my window that wasn't Steve." She took a deep breath, reliving the events in her head. "I decided to go check things out, so I grabbed the gun and went to the back door. When I got there, I could hear a weird noise that was really creepy. I turned on the porch light and opened the blinds at the same time." Her palms became sweaty, and her heart pounded at the memory of the ordeal.

John tensed, stiffening, and held her closer to him. As concerned as he was with what she would reveal next, he could barely breathe.

After taking a deep breath, she let it out, telling him, "What I saw...the guy had stabbed Steve and he was lying there bleeding all over the place and trying to breathe. And the man...he looked crazy and downright scary when he saw me. He ran towards me.

When he started running at me, I shot him. He was fast though. He actually made it almost to the door before I shot him."

When she finished, they lay together in silence for a while staring into each other's eyes. Somehow, she knew that although he wouldn't condemn her for the murder, he would be hell-bent on protecting her.

He was the first to move. Placing his hand on her hip and squeezing, he embraced her. After turning her to face him, he kissed her softly and slowly. After a moment, the kiss deepened as he rolled on top of her, spreading her legs. He bit her lip, following it with a swipe of his tongue which had her moaning into his mouth. Having fallen asleep without dressing, the two were skin to skin. She grinded against him as they continued to kiss. His erection lay between them, leaving pearl-colored drops on both of their abdomens.

Wanting to feel more of his nips and his mouth, she directed his face to her breasts. He obliged her, causing her to cry out, "Oh John!" and grind against him again. He took his cue and lifted himself while spreading her legs further. Then he slammed into her, causing her to cry out once more. After thrusting himself into her repeatedly and building the fire for both of them, he pulled back and held himself still just inside her. Feeling deprived, she worked to fully impale herself, but he would not relent.

"I want to see your face flushed with passion," he teased her.

She moaned, still trying to force him all the way inside, but he held her hips without budging. "Please," was all she managed to get out between her gasps for air.

He smiled down at her, taking pleasure in how much she wanted him. Finally, he demanded, "Tell me that you want me buried deep inside you, Morgan, and I will give you what you need."

She struggled, barely able to hold onto a thought, let alone form a complete, coherent sentence. "Please, John," she stammered, sure she would go up in flames at any moment. When he remained still, she renewed her effort to have him fully inside her, but to no effect.

"Say it, *ma shearc*," he entreated her, "and this will be yours." He thrust into her once, attempting to tease the words from her that he was so determined to hear.

Her head turned from side to side and she moaned, needing desperately to find release. She again pleaded, "Please John, I need you deep inside me."

Smiling triumphantly, he began pistoning into her, again building the fire for both of them. Finally she exploded, seeing stars as John's orgasm erupted, spewing jets into her. Spent, he collapsed on top of her.

Unable to move, they lay together, still connected. Finally, after taking a deep breath, he repositioned himself to look down at her face as he observed, "You had a very close call, *ma shearc*. Why did you not call me?"

Morgan gathered her courage, concerned that their conversation was heading toward a place she wanted to avoid. Finally, she countered his question. "Call you? Why would I have called you at that point?" she asked, reminding him that their love affair with each other had only just begun.

Nodding his head, he acquiesced to her statement, but then passionately whispered, "I cannot abide this, my little doll. I cannot lose you." Reaching out, he tucked a section of stray hairs behind her ear.

"You will not lose me. I'm too stubborn to die," she assured him. "And besides, the two that wanted to hurt me are dead."

He mulled over her words for a moment as she traced the lines of his lower lip with the pad of her thumb. When he finally spoke, it was a strong plea that bordered on command. "Move in with me."

Shocked by his request, Morgan had difficulty pulling air into her lungs and felt dizzy for a moment.

Finally, she incredulously exclaimed, "Are you crazy?!"

He withdrew from her abruptly, and then sat up, looking like she'd slapped his face. "Why not?" he demanded.

Morgan was stunned by his request, and she couldn't understand how he could even consider such a ridiculous suggestion. Sitting up and planting herself in front of him, she exclaimed, "That's an awful idea! No offense, but do you really think it would be smart of us to move in together right now?"

He crossed his arms over his chest and looked at her angrily before saying one of the last things she expected. "You should go now."

Morgan felt like he had struck her. "Excuse me?!" she demanded incredulously. "You don't like what I have to say so you want me to leave?"

"No," he retorted coldly. "You refuse to allow me to keep you safe. You are obviously a person in need of protection. If I cannot protect you then I fear I will lose you, and that would be more painful than I could bear. Better that you leave now before I become too attached."

The stubborn set of his jaw told her that John would likely not change his mind, but that didn't stop her from loudly expressing her opinion. "Of all the

dumb things to say!" she exclaimed, exasperated.
"I'm not saying you're dumb, but you are being really
stupid about this. I have remained alive without you
for the last thirty-four years of my life. What makes
you think that unless I all of the sudden up and move
in with you, I will be hurt or killed?"

A startling conclusion found its way into her
brain. "Wait," she said. "Are you saying that you
won't see me anymore if I don't move in with you?"

His eyes brightened before he spoke, as if he
expected her to change her mind. "I am saying that
if you will not be where I can protect you, I will not
continue this relationship with you." As he made this
declaration, he rubbed her calf, hoping to make her
understand his concern and agree to live with him.

Morgan watched as his fingers stroked a
circular pattern, and for a moment allowed herself to
get lost in the sensation. Sitting quietly, she turned his
words over in her mind, processing the ultimatum.
"I love the feel of you touching me, and of you inside
me, John…and just the thought of your mouth on
me almost makes me cum." As she quietly made the
admission, she watched his fingers hypnotically.

Taking a deep breath and gathering her
resolve, she looked him in the eye and said, "I cannot
live with you right now. It's impossible."

His fingers stopped. He withdrew his hands, placing them in his lap.

"There is nothing more to say then. You may go."

John's words hurt more than any physical blow he could've dealt her, and she felt shaky as she scooted away from him. Without saying a word and without looking at him, Morgan quickly dressed herself and then left. To her surprise, she made it all the way to her car before the deluge of tears began.

Chapter Three

As the sun began its daily journey across the sky, Maggie sat up and stretched, yawning until the tiredness crept away. Hearing her mother's breathing machine go off for the third time, she rolled her eyes and jumped out of bed, moving toward the sound. She was not prepared for what she saw at her mother's bedside.

Gasping for breath and with blue lips, her mom stared at her as if from a faraway distance. Mag immediately went to work checking the tubes for patency. When she could find no blockage and the machines were in working order, she started resuscitating her mom while simultaneously hitting the emergency call button.

After several moments of chest compressions, the light returned to her mother's eyes and she began choking, until she expelled what seemed like a liter of mucus. As the coughing spell continued, Mag heard the doorbell ring. Running to the door, she let the paramedics in. While they took over, she collapsed onto the sofa in a daze, staring into space while the paramedics started an IV and connected new tubes.

Maggie's stupor was interrupted by one of the medics shaking her shoulder and repeating, "Ma'am, are you the daughter?"

She blinked and looked up at him. "Yes! I'm her daughter."

She looked over at her mother, who was being wheeled out, while the medic brought her up to speed. "We got her stabilized. She's satting okay right now: in the high 80's. We're taking her to OU Medical Center. Would you like to ride along, or will you be following?"

Mag snapped out of her reverie and announced, "I will ride along," as she moved toward the ambulance.

****

At the Emergency Department, Miss Sumner was taken to a room where they intubated her and began collecting labs. The staff wouldn't allow Maggie to be with her mother until they stabilized her, and she lingered helplessly in the waiting room. Pacing anxiously, she looked expectantly to every new person that entered, hoping for news of her mother's health.

Finally, she was approached by a man in a white lab coat. "Are you Miss Sumner?" he asked. She nodded, and he waved for her to follow him.

To her surprise, she was led to a bank of elevators next to the waiting room. Once inside, the doctor turned to her. "Your mom is really sick. We've moved her to the ICU." He paused for a moment, as if gauging her reaction. She took a deep breath, nodding, and he continued, "I'm sorry to be the one to tell you this, but it would take a miracle for her to live through the night."

Maggie couldn't breathe after hearing the news. She tried to suck air into her lungs, but it just wasn't happening.

"Are you okay, Miss?" he asked. When she gave no response, he put his hand on the back of her neck and applied slight pressure, prompting her to lean forward. "That's it. Breathe," he instructed her.

When the elevator abruptly stopped, she lost her footing. Thankfully, he braced her to prevent her from falling forward. She felt stunned, and time seemed to stop. Finally, a wheelchair appeared out of nowhere, and the doctor helped her to sit down.

Before long, she was parked next to her mother's bed staring at what looked like a corpse. "Oh, Mom!" she cried out. She grabbed her mother's pale hand and held it to her own face. There was no response or recognition as Maggie kissed the hand.

After sitting with her mother for a while, a woman came in and introduced herself as the hospital chaplain. "I'm very sorry to meet you under these circumstances," she told Maggie in a somber tone.

Mag looked up at her, coming to a realization: the chaplain's presence indicated that her mother wasn't likely to live much longer. Silent tears began to stream down her face. After setting a packet on the bedside table, the chaplain left as quietly as she had entered. Maggie sat soundlessly and waited. Finally, needing support desperately, she phoned her best friend.

When she connected with Morgan, she could do nothing but sob into the handset. While Morgan wouldn't recognize the number from the hospital phone, she obviously recognized the voice. "Maggie? What is it, Maggie? What's wrong?!" Morgan asked, sounding alarmed.

"Mom...hospital...OU...dying," she barely managed to get out, each word accentuated with a sob.

"I'm on the way, Mags. I'll be there. Hold on. I'm only five minutes from you."

****

Dr. Schambaugh concluded his rounds by seeing the woman in 2182 who was dying from complications of multiple sclerosis. He had wanted to save the most intense visit for last; it didn't do to get caught up in emotions when you were making medical decisions that affected people's lives. In his work, control was an important factor. When you carried the power of life and death in your hands, you had to maintain that control at all times.

In fact, it was with no small amount of control that he approached the grieving daughter. She was quietly crying. She was also beautiful, as well as subdued, he observed. This woman, he concluded, was especially good at controlling herself.

"You gonna be the one to tell her?" Big Bertha asked.

Big Bertha was the heavy-set black nurse whose antics Dr. Schambaugh tolerated. He was not, in fact, at all disappointed to talk to the lovely redhead in mourning. Playing the game, he murmured, "Yes. I would be happy to help the damsel in distress," as he walked into the ICU bay.

Maggie Sumner looked up as Dr. Schambaugh walked in, obviously collecting herself in preparation for bad news. Attempting to appear confident and self-possessed, he could tell that she expected the worst.

"Hello, Miss Sumner, I'm Dr. Schambaugh, the neurology Fellow." Miss Sumner nodded her head in acknowledgment, holding her breath. "I heard how your mom is doing and I wanted to personally come by and discuss her care with you."

Just then, a dark-haired woman walked in and went straight to Miss Sumner, pulling her in for a warm embrace. Dr Schambaugh observed the two women quietly while they made their exchange.

"I'm so sorry Maggie. How are you holding up?" the newcomer inquired.

Miss Sumner sobbed silently into her friend's shoulder for a few moments, and then lifted her head and wiped her face. "I'm better now that you're here," she said. She then turned to Dr. Schambaugh, awaiting information concerning her mom's fate.

He restarted his introduction for the new arrival. "Hi. I'm Dr. Schambaugh, the neurology Fellow. Sorry you're going through this, and sorry to meet under these circumstances." They both nodded, and he continued. "I was reviewing your mom's recent health record. It says she received most of her care of late at home from you?"

"Yes," Miss Sumner confirmed. "I've been taking care of her needs. Hospital care is so expensive, and I wanted her to remain in the comfort of her own home for as long as possible."

The doctor considered her words for a moment, and then asked, "Where on earth did you learn…that is, how did you know how to care for her?"

She immediately assumed a defensive stance. "Excuse me?!" she demanded.

He was taken aback by her seeming outrage at his question, but then surmised that she was likely experiencing guilt regarding her mother's declined state of health. Filing that away for later, he hurried on with an explanation. "I wondered because the level of deterioration with her MS…with the lesions…they are the most severe I have ever seen in a living person." He paused for a moment to allow the information to sink in. "You must have taken extremely good care of her in order for her to have survived for so long."

The doctor's validation was obviously a big relief to the guilt-stricken woman. She had likely been thinking that had she done something differently, her mother wouldn't be in her dire situation. After taking a deep breath, he finished, "So where did you learn how to give medical care?"

She cleared her throat of tears and said, "I'm an LPN at an LTAC." Her friend was rubbing the beautiful redhead's shoulders as the conversation took place; likely, he thought, to comfort her.

"I'm impressed," he observed. "You're a miracle worker. I don't know of many RN's, or doctors for that matter, who could've kept your mom alive as long as you have. I'm interested in discussing the care you gave her at some point in the future when things settle down. Can I take you to lunch sometime?"

Her dark-haired friend suddenly stopped the massage, obviously surprised at the request. Her expression darkened briefly, as if she suspected that he was hitting on her grieving friend, but then cleared a moment later as she likely ascribed any such concerns to her own imagination.

Miss Sumner…Maggie…also appeared stunned by the request. Regardless, she agreed to the lunch date, even if only to honor her dedication to nursing and to help others by sharing her experience. Having gotten what he'd come for, Dr Schambaugh quickly explained the prognosis, stating that he didn't expect her to live through the next couple of nights. He then quietly withdrew from the room, giving the two women some privacy.

While Morgan thought the doctor was kind enough in his attentiveness to Mag's plight, there was something about him that didn't sit right with her. She couldn't put her finger on it. Before she could examine it too closely, however, he was gone and her friend was asking her to call her brother as well as her other family members. She quickly agreed.

After the phone calls had been made, Maggie needed to get some air and asked Morgan to accompany her outside. While loitering by the waterfall that was situated in one corner of the vast medical complex, Maggie lit a cigarette and breathed it out with a long exhale. Turning, she said, "I'm so glad you're here, Morgan. I don't know what I would do if you weren't."

Morgan was Maggie's oldest friend. She kissed her best friend on the lips and said, "I wouldn't be anywhere else but here, Mags. I love you so much. I'm so sorry this is happening."

Maggie really looked at her for the first time since her arrival, narrowing her eyes. "What's going on with you, Morgy?" Flicking her cigarette into the pond, she waited for an answer.

Morgan's heart jumped and her face became flushed. She should have known that her best friend would sense her turbulent emotions. She didn't want to discuss her heartbreak with anyone at the present time, however. Aside from the fact that Mag was going through such a horrible situation, Morgan still hadn't had time to process her own ordeal which had transpired just that morning.

Hiding her face, she lied, "I'm fine. I just...I'm in shock with your mom. I mean I knew this could happen and I knew she was sick. I guess it's just easy to take for granted that a person you love, who has always been there, will always be there."

She hoped her partial truth would pass Mag's lie detector test; but when Mag continued to stare at her with narrowed eyes, Morgan realized she wasn't buying it.

"Bullshit. Don't lie to me," Maggie said warningly. "I know I've got this with my mom and all, but don't shut me out of what's going on with you. You know I can smell your lies from a mile away."

Morgan was afraid her friend would push despite what was going on in her own life, but she wasn't sure that she should tell Maggie about the still-fresh ordeal of that morning and preceding evening. When she was still hesitant, Maggie persuaded her by explaining, "Look, I've known for a while that my mom was getting close to dying. It's still hard of course, and I'm very thankful to Dr. Schambaugh for explaining to me that I did a good job in caring for her."

She took a deep breath before continuing the explanation in greater detail. "You see, when I woke up and saw my mom looking the way she did, I felt awful. I felt like I hadn't done enough to keep her alive." When Morgan started to protest, she cut her off. "You don't have to say it. I know. And talking to the doc about it settles it. So I'm fine on that front. But don't you shut me out. In fact, hearing about someone else's problems will probably help keep my mind off of my mom for a while."

Morgan took a deep breath. Before she could stop herself, the tears began to flow and she started sobbing. Maggie embraced and soothed her until the storm subsided. Eventually, Morgan straightened herself, wiping her eyes and face. Then she took a cleansing breath and started to share her tale. She didn't know quite where to begin. She opened her mouth, and then closed it. Maggie knew her very well, and therefore sat quietly and patiently, allowing Morgan to collect her thoughts.

After a moment, she began, "So this crazy guy was stalking me for a few weeks. It was a short time really, because he got so worked up so fast." She paused a moment, deciding where to go next. "Well, Steve came back around that time too. Jerk!"

Though she had heard it was bad luck to talk poorly of the dead, she couldn't help but respond to the anger she still felt at his recent behavior. Stifling the urge to rant on about him, she chose to continue. "So I added security cameras and some other stuff at the house because of McCrazy Stalker, and oh yeah, I bought some guns."

Maggie gasped, knowing how much Morgan opposed firearms. In answer, Morgan said, "I know I always hated them, but this asshole made it personal. He was talking about coming after my family... my kids. I'll be fucking damned if I'm going to take that bullshit lying down. So I got the guns and Mack helped install the extra cameras. Then I did safety drills with the kids."

After taking another deep breath, she proceeded, "Well, I'm glad I did all of that. Monday night...luckily the kids were gone because my mom took them to Disney World. I'd taken Lortab and like an idiot, drank some wine. But I woke up in the middle of the night because I could hear someone outside my window. I looked at the surveillance camera and fucking Steve was out there, so I called 911."

She gained a sense of relief from sharing the story with her friend. "I was on the phone for a few minutes explaining where he was to dispatch, so I wasn't sure where he went. But when I looked back on the camera I saw something...another person. I couldn't see what he looked like. It was dark, and he was wearing black, so I couldn't see his face." She had to stop for a moment to gather her thoughts again.

"I grabbed my gun and got it ready. I walked to the back door and I could hear a strange sound. I wasn't sure what it was then, but I knew I had to find out what was going on in the backyard, and I had to do it so that I could protect myself while at the same time seeing what was happening." With this statement, her speech slowed, as though she had to relive it in order to tell it accurately.

"I opened the blinds and turned on the porch light at the same time. I saw...Steve lying in front of the door...covered in blood. He was surrounded by blood that was everywhere. So much that I didn't even know a body could hold that much of it. But I saw that only very briefly, because I had to look around to see who else was out there.

"It didn't take me long at all to see the other guy. He was standing in the grass right where the porch ends. As soon as he saw me, he kinda went crazy. I mean really, he looked like a wild animal. Then he lunged at me…at the back door toward me. I'm not sure how long that whole thing took…it seems like it took forever, but it had to be really quick. I didn't think. I didn't second-guess myself. I just raised the gun and shot him. A whole bunch of times."

Morgan stopped to take a deep breath before continuing. "He died of course…prophet or not, which is what he claimed to be. And I tried to help Steve. He was stabbed in the neck. I held my hand there for a while, putting pressure on the wound, like I remembered you talking about from nursing school. But it was just too deep, and he didn't make it."

Maggie listened to all of this in stunned silence while Morgan finished her story. When Morgan volunteered nothing further, she finally asked, "Okay, then what? Did something else happen?"

Morgan was shocked that her friend knew her so well; Maggie could obviously sense that the bombshell she had just received was not her only source of distress.

She had to gather herself for a long time, and realized that she was probably stalling when Maggie insisted, "I'm not going to let it go, so you may as well tell me."

Morgan had to smile at her friend's stubborn persistence. "I don't know how I ever let you in so far that you never let me get away with anything, but you're right." Her smile faded at the last of her words, and her face became a mask of intense sorrow as the tears began again. Maggie seemed to sense that she needed a moment and waited patiently for Morgan to prepare herself.

Finally, she was ready, and said, "You know the couple I told you about that I saw a couple of times?" Maggie briefly nodded in acknowledgment. "I wanted to see them again, and we *did* see each other. But things kicked up a notch not long after I last talked to you. I didn't mean for it to. It was just sex at first…really good sex. But they were married, so in a way, I think I thought it was safer. Kind of like the reason people have affairs with married people sometimes. They just think there's less of a chance of getting their heart deeply involved…they feel safer and less vulnerable.

"I think that's what I thought for a while. But there was an intense attraction between John and me. His wife and I were way into each other also, but I started realizing that something wasn't right between the two of them. I discounted it because it was still the three of us in this rendezvous, and we had a great time together. They were good to each other at first for the most part…until Friday when it all changed."

Morgan had to stop for a moment to decide how much she would disclose, but then carried on, "I had an appointment to show the house across from theirs and I didn't realize it was actually his brother that was interested. When I showed up, his brother scared the shit out of me. I had gotten a shit ton of awful emails from McCrazy, and the brother looked really angry when I first saw him. But then John was right there and he let me know it was his brother and not some crazy ass stalker. After that, I gave Patrick-that's his brother- a tour of the house.

"But while John and I were alone together in the house we...we...it was so hot. So awful to do behind Jasmine's back, but it was so hot." She paused to gauge Mag's reaction. Her face was open, so Morgan continued. "We were in the bathroom. We were kissing and we had our hands all over each other. I've never felt so desired by another person in my entire life. But then I stopped it because I didn't want to do that to Jasmine.

"But he said or did something that was really hot, and we went back at it again, and it was going hot and heavy for a while. But then he stopped it. He helped me dress and straighten my clothes, and he had me go out and occupy his brother. 'I cannot go out in this condition', he said in his thick accent." She imitated him animatedly, while explaining her account of events.

"So I went out and we all finished the tour. Afterwards, we went across the street to John's house and told his wife what we'd done. I thought she would be angry with us. I thought our affair was over. Instead, she said she was happy that we were so into each other. It was so weird because I really do believe she was happy for us. And she wanted us to all three get together again like we were celebrating our lust for each other."

Morgan started fidgeting, knowing that she was about to disclose some difficult information. "So we did our thing together…the three of us. And it was great like always." Catching her breath again, she had to take a break for a moment; Maggie waited patiently like always. Composure regained, Morgan continued. "It was really good. I think we all really enjoyed it. But when John's wife orgasmed, she called out his brother's name."

Maggie let out a quick gasp that escaped before she could stop it. To recover, she said, "Oh my. I can't believe she did that. Was John furious with her?"

Morgan confirmed with a nod, and then said, "I've never seen him so angry before. I was worried he was going to actually physically assault her for a second. But I could see the hurt in his eyes also.

"Jasmine looked like she was really surprised that it slipped out; and she looked like she was really sorry for saying it. I think she was. I really think they were trying to work things out, which is why they originally called me. But there are some things that are impossible to put behind you, and the heart loves who it loves. The mind may have other ideas, but in the end the heart almost always has its way."

Speaking this truth was empowering for Morgan, and it gave her a burst of energy that helped her to keep going. "After he heard her say that, he basically told her that he would forgive her and let it go if she would give him time alone with me. I didn't feel right about it even though I wanted him so badly. But I couldn't stand the idea of helping him 'punish' her…I really like her and I'm thankful that she has been so generous with herself and with him. Plus I felt kinda bad for her because he was so angry with her."

She cleared her throat before continuing. "She practically begged me…said it would mean a lot to her. I felt like it was the only way to redeem her situation. So I agreed and she left. But not before thanking me like I'd thrown her a lifeline.

"And then John and I…it was amazing. I couldn't even call it sex. We made love. It was amazing. The way he touches me…it's like he really listens to me. He pays attention to what my body tells him, and he remembers the way my body responds the best. He wants to know how to pleasure me. I've never had a lover like him." It was apparent that there was a "but" in there, and Maggie sensed that it wasn't related to Morgan's lover's marital status.

"I saw him this morning," Morgan announced after a long pause. "I'd just left him when you called me." Maggie started to look remorseful, but Morgan halted it. "He told me to leave."

The tears were threatening to start up again, and Morgan swallowed several times before hurrying on. "His wife called me yesterday, saying that she wanted to talk to me about something that concerned me. I was really curious of course, though a little nervous. I hadn't talked to her since John and I had our lone session. But I met with her to see what she had in mind.

"Jasmine told me about how she and John met, which was, in many ways, tragic. I won't go into details…it's her story to tell. But she quickly fell in love with John's brother. I don't think she knows if she ever really loved John. But she and Patrick fell in love. Their affair went on for some time until John caught them, and then it was over."

Understanding registered on Maggie's face, and Morgan persevered. "So they tried to reconcile by bringing me into their lovemaking. I think they thought I would help to rekindle the love that had once been there. But it was too far gone from what I can tell. Instead of rekindling their love, I sparked something in John. And I reminded Jasmine of what she once had with Patrick, but has lost."

When Morgan remained silent for a while, Maggie reminded her that she was working toward a point. "So what happened this morning?"

Snapping out of her reverie, Morgan trudged on. "Jasmine told me all about their problems last night, and I could tell that she was leading up to something…some kind of proposal. When I asked, she told me that she thought John and I were better for each other, and that she and Patrick were more suited to be together. I was shocked of course, and I couldn't believe John would agree to it, so I asked. She said he was thinking about it." Morgan could see that Maggie was surprised by the development, and she waited a moment to let the news sink in.

Finally she continued, "I was really intrigued by the idea of having John to myself, but a part of me didn't believe it, and after lunch with Jasmine I called him. He wanted me to come to his hotel so that we could talk about it. He even had a room close to where we ate lunch, so I went over there."

Blushing, she recounted their reunion. "We didn't actually talk much then…we couldn't keep our hands off of each other. It's almost like we have a compulsion when we're around each other and we can't *not* touch, and we can't *not* have really hot, passionate sex.

"That was last night. This morning we woke up, and when he asked what I planned to do today, I ended up telling him about Steve and McCrazy."

Mag's eyes widened, and she demanded, "Holy shit! What did he say?"

Morgan smiled, enjoying the infusion of enthusiasm that helped to pep up the tone of the conversation, and then answered. "Well, nothing at first. Actually, he said I had a close call and that it scared him…and then we had phenomenal sex." Morgan's big smile and blush seemed to put Maggie at ease for a moment, although it was obvious to both that there was still a devastating component of the interaction to discuss.

"The sex," Morgan admitted, "was so amazing. You know how most of the time when a guy cums…" Morgan had to stop herself as she remembered that her best friend was actually grossly inexperienced in the area of sexual partners. "I'm sorry Maggie," she empathized. Mag shooed her condolences away and prompted her to continue. Morgan made a mental note to get her friend laid, and then finished her tale of woe.

"So guys can be boneheads in bed. Most of them, at least the ones I've been with, orgasm, and then don't give two shits if you finish. John is a very generous lover. He has always made sure I orgasm when we have been together. And like I said, it seems like he has paid attention from the beginning to learn what my body likes and how I respond best. Just thinking about it makes me wet," she announced, blushing again and grinning for a moment.

Morgan collected her thoughts before telling her best friend about her source of sorrow. "So the sex this morning…it was…I find myself wanting to call it something that would make it like a gift from God, but it doesn't seem right to place having sex with a married man in that class. But it was so amazing!

"But then the bottom dropped out. He practically demanded that I move in with him, saying that it's the only way for him to protect me."

Mag's mouth dropped open and she exclaimed, "What the fuck! Was he on drugs you didn't know about?"

Morgan agreed with her. "I know; that's what I said. I actually asked him if he's crazy. And I tried to talk him out of that little idea of his, but he wouldn't hear it.

"Eventually, he said he couldn't stand to lose me but would rather it happen now than when he becomes more attached. He rationalized that if I won't let him protect me, then I'll get hurt or killed, so I may as well go now before he gets too close."

Maggie's outrage was evident; she was pissed on behalf of her friend. "How can he possibly think that's a good idea," she demanded. Morgan nodded and then cleared her throat. "What?" her friend asked, "There's more?"

Morgan closed her eyes for a moment before answering, knowing that the next statement would hurt the most. "I told him I was in love with him for the first time last night." She had to choke back tears at the rejection and pain she felt from her admission. Maggie would understand why that part was so painful, and she hugged her friend.

The two continued to embrace while they each sobbed silently into the other's shoulder. After a long cry, the two women each gave a shuddering sigh and then collected themselves. "We should go back in and check on your mom," Morgan told her friend. They hugged one last time and then returned to the ICU.

Chapter Four

John watched his lover go from the bed that he was lying sprawled out and naked on. Through half-lidded eyes, he tracked her as she gathered her things and prepared to leave. After the door slammed shut, he groaned and had to shake the urge to cry.

Analyzing the conversation that had taken place, he assured himself that she would come back. Every time Jasmine refused one of his demands, she went away for several hours, but then returned to do what he asked. It was, he figured, a game women liked to play. So he would not cry. He would remain strong until she complied with his wishes. He just didn't understand why he had such a sinking feeling in his gut.

Packing his things, he decided that going home to his children was the wisest thing to do. If he had to wait on his woman to make up her mind, spending time with his daughters was the best idea. And he could see how his wife was doing with getting Patrick to make up his mind.

The idea of his wife with his younger brother set his teeth on edge. It was one thing for his wife not to show loyalty to him; at one time he had expected nothing less. But that was before their big conversation. She may even have been correct when she convinced him of their need to pursue the love of others. But he had difficulty excusing the betrayal of his own flesh and blood. He wasn't sure that he would ever be able to forgive Patrick.

He cut off that line of thought when he arrived at the front desk to check out. "Was your stay absolutely sensuous?" The front desk girl asked, feigning embarrassment, before continuing, "Oh. My bad, I meant *satisfactory*," she corrected, and smiled at him enticingly.

He could see that she was baiting him, and he decided to take what she offered. Giving her the most charming smile he could muster, he leaned against the counter and openly leered at her breasts which were easily visible: the top of her blouse barely covered her nipples, which were quite perky.

"It could've been better," he stated, using his thick accent to seduce her more effectively. Her answering blush was all he needed to proceed, and he prompted her, "Do you get breaks around here very often?" as he pretended to covertly grope his crotch. She perked up and yelled for one of her co-workers- a short fat man-child that John hadn't noticed before.

"Glen," she yelled, "this guest would like me to show him around. I need you to work the front desk." The man-boy she called Glen seemed to be enthralled with her, and gladly took her place at the counter, ignorant to the fact that the guest she was professing to help was about to give it to her good and hard.

Following her up the stairs, John was led to a bathroom on the second floor. Once they were both inside, she quickly secured the lock. Right away, she turned to him and started stroking his muscular chest. He grabbed her by the wrists and pushed her away from him, turning her around.

"How do you like it from behind?" he asked her, as his hand ascended her thigh and he yanked on her panties. They landed silently, wrapped around her ankles.

"As long as I can look at you in the mirror while you do it," she said, looking at his reflection over her shoulder. He gladly complied as he slipped a condom on and then entered her. Her answering moan told him she enjoyed it, and he reached his arm around to stroke her while he moved inside of her.

She froze for a moment, not seeming to like him fondling her. "Just fuck me!" she demanded, glaring at him in the mirror. Eventually, he resumed, propelling himself into her. After several moments, her hips began to move more frantically. Suddenly she cried out...and then stood on her toes and was still.

He thought she might have orgasmed, but wasn't sure; Jasmine always rode him hard and long, and in his experience women took longer. As he wasn't finished, he continued to pound into her. She stood still for a few more moments, taking what he gave her. But then he noticed her glaring at him again.

As his rhythm slowed, she pushed him away with her elbows. "I just wanted a quick screw, but I had to pick the energizer fucking bunny!" she swore. "Well at least I got off. Thank you for that, but next time don't do me any goddamn favors."

With that, she stormed out, and John was left holding onto his penis. Choosing to make the most of it, he decided to jerk himself off; this time, he thought of Morgan, and came very quickly, shooting his wad all over the sink and onto the mirror.

As he walked out, he chuckled to himself, thinking about the mess he was leaving. He hoped that bitch at the front desk checked the bathroom later. He wanted her to feel humiliated as she had made him feel humiliated.

****

After arriving at home, John stopped in the kitchen to say hello to his mother and kiss her on the cheek. She was in her usual foul mood, and complained to him about his being out all night the previous evening. She also griped about Jasmine and asked John to have a talk with his 'Little Princess Wife' about her poor mothering skills.

John chose to intervene on his wife's behalf. Flustered, he looked his mother directly in the eye and said, "I understand that you two have your differences, but do not forget that she is my wife, and the mother of your grandchildren. And I want you to remember that when you say hurtful things about her, you're punishing not only her but also the kids and me."

Brunne appeared taken aback; not only by his reprimand, but also at his defense of his wife. It was no surprise, since of late, John and Jasmine had hardly been civil to each other. It was possible also that Brunne knew about the illicit affair between Jasmine and Patrick.

With a slight nod, she conceded that John had a point. She then stated hesitantly, "Ye are right, o' course, me dear, and I do apologize fer speaking ill of ye're beautiful wife. It's just tha' she ha' filled the wee ones heids wi' the idea of ye puttin' in a pool. Ye know how I feel about..." She trailed off, as he sighed and rubbed his eyes.

"Mother, must I have this conversation with you again? You know I am careful with our money, and as I told you the last time, what I spend now is what I earned from investing in the Stock Market. The original family fortune is right where it belongs, in the safe at home."

Brunne looked remorseful for the first time in as long as he could remember. It was confirmed when she patted his shoulder and sheepishly smiled, and then stated, "I know this, me dear boy, and me thinks ye have done an excellent job of handling the family's fortune. I jus' worry about ye sometimes. And I love Jasmine, but I worry sometimes that the lass is unfulfilled and spends ye're money as a way to handle yon burdens."

Brunne appeared taken aback as the words left her mouth. John studied his mother for a few moments, considering her words, and wondered just how much of the inner workings his mother had sensed during the past several months. Initially he was insulted by her nosiness, irritated that she seemed to be constantly in a bad mood, and steadily ready to complain about any perceived slight. But as he remembered the tiresome life his mother had led, and the burdens she had suffered at her children's' expense, he thought better of it.

After taking a deep breath and then hugging her, he made an unusual request. "Ma, will you make some of the soda bread you used to make for me when I was but a lad?"

Brunne appeared stunned at his request. John mused that she was likely touched that her son wanted something she had made during his childhood. His suspicions were confirmed when she swiped at the tears that made their way down her wizened cheeks, and hugged him tightly. "Me precious boy, of course I will make that for ya! I love ye so. Even though ye're nigh on forty, ye will always be me wee one."

The sudden embrace, along with the sight of tears on his beloved mother's face nearly moved John to tears, which he covered by turning his face into her hair. "Ma, I will always be your baby, as you have often told me. I love you very much. Even when you grouse at me so." His statement ended with him kissing her on the forehead, and mother and son smiling lovingly at each other.

After a moment of silence, he announced, "I will be in my office, if you need anything, ma." With that, he made his way to the heavy oak door that led into his sanctuary, as his mother gave a heartwarming smile, and then began busying herself, in preparation of the treat she would make for her beloved firstborn.

In his office, John sat quiet and still, eventually realizing that he'd been staring into space for some time. As he attempted to define the source of his distraction, his mind turned to Morgan.

Looking down at his desk, he smiled as he remembered what he had done when he'd last sat there. He swiftly removed his pants as his arousal grew, and went to work stroking himself.

Already hard, he closed his eyes and pictured Morgan's mouth on him. As he licked his lips, he imagined her flavor on his tongue. Then, remembering that he'd fondled the front desk girl a short while ago, he brought his fingers to his nose and sniffed. Unexpectedly repelled by the fishy scent, his erection quickly deflated. After a quick search, he located his stash of bleach wipes, and used them to remove the offending odor from his fingertips. After trashing the tissues, he closed his eyes and wondered if it would ever be the same without Morgan, preparing himself for the possibility that she would not return.

****

Upstairs, Jasmine had just laid the girls down for their afternoon nap. She'd heard John's voice earlier and knew that he was home. Wishing to avoid him, she left the nursery and went outside for some fresh air. As she surveyed their yard, her mind daydreamed about the times Patrick had stayed with them, when they had made love repeatedly under the large oak tree. It was not long after that first rendezvous that John had discovered their affair.

She strolled to that favorite of trees, studying the ground beneath, picturing a garden there. It was one of the most serene places in the yard, and for her it symbolized the peace that she felt when she and Patrick were together. So ironic, considering that an affair typically meant more stress while with one's lover. She sighed as she lay down under the spreading branches of the tree that held such fond memories.

Studying the sky through the branches, Jasmine thought back to the first time she'd lain in this spot, with Patrick gloriously inside her, worshipping her body with his. It was right around this time three years ago, she mused. An elusive thought slipped through her mind, threatening to leave before she could fully capture it. Trying to recover it, she looked over at the trunk of the tree, and then back at the cool February sky through the leaves and branches. As she studied the clouds, the idea snapped back into the forefront of her mind.

She thought about the length of an average pregnancy. She then considered the date of her last backyard encounter with Patrick. Performing a quick calculation, her heart skipped a beat. *Callista's birthday is November 2nd,* she thought. She couldn't believe that she hadn't figured this out previously, but the dates matched; Patrick could be, and likely was, her youngest child's father.

Further, Callie looked just like Patrick, even having his mild temperament and sense of humor. As she worked over the details in her mind, her shock turned to elation. Though she felt selfish for wishing it a reality, part of her *wanted* Patrick as the father of her child. The idea of a part of him growing inside of her body made her feel immensely satisfied, and she was warm at the thought.

Pushing herself up off of the ground, she reflected on her revelation as she walked toward the house. Once inside, she took a sharp right into John's office. Closing the door behind her, she found herself confronted by the sight of her husband vigorously stroking himself. Dumbfounded, she stood and watched. The intensity with which he thrust himself into his own hand, coupled by the look of deep concentration on his face, suggested that he was having difficulty achieving an orgasm.

When he looked at her, his shaft immediately deflated. He slowly covered himself with a towel, glaring at her as though she was the cause of his erection dysfunction.

"Shall I call Morgan to help you with that?" she offered, only partially joking.

John pulled the towel away and aggressively waved his flaccid organ at her. "Or you could do for me what any good wife would do." Then, as an afterthought, he retorted, "Even if you are in love with my brother."

Jasmine studied him with amusement for a moment as he handled his prized member, her smile fading as she realized that he was serious. "Do you really mean that?" she asked, trying to understand his intentions as she watched him closely. He held his arm out to her, gesturing for her to join him. She stared at him for one brief moment, and then took what he offered.

Sitting behind his desk in his office chair, John pulled her onto his lap. He wrapped her palm around his stiffening member and proceeded to stroke himself with her hand. She looked down at the way he was using her, and found herself extremely turned on by watching him pleasure himself through her.

"Shall I?" she asked, as she suggestively motioned with her chin toward his crotch.

John's cock jumped in anticipation and became semi-erect, almost as if it had a mind of its own. He smiled and then picked his wife up from his lap, placing her on the floor before him, almost under the desk.

"Mmmmm, Jasmine. I have always enjoyed the feel of your mouth on me." As he settled himself back in the chair, her mouth enveloped him. He began to thrust rhythmically into her mouth…until the door to the kitchen opened, heralding the appearance of his mother.

John instantly froze, likely thankful for the desk, as it hid Jasmine from view. He tried to look disinterested as his mother asked him about food preferences. Throughout the conversation, Jasmine– behaving mischievously, with a wicked gleam in her eyes– continued her ministrations, provoking a light squirm from her husband. It likely seemed like hours to John that his mother discussed mundane details of baking with him while his wife did desirable things to him below, just out of sight. In all actuality, the conversation lasted only a handful of minutes.

When his mother finally left, John exploded into Jasmine's mouth, and she grinned triumphantly, releasing him. He would not leave things there, however; not after the havoc she had caused. He pulled her back onto his lap and whispered in her ear, "You are going to pay for that, you little tease," punctuating the last with a friendly nip of her earlobe.

He then stood, bringing Jasmine to her feet. Determinedly, he bent her over his desk and removed her clothing from the waist down. Leaning down over her prostrate form, he whispered, "I do not mind if you call me Patrick. This is our last fuck for old time's sake.

He then entered her with a force that had his balls slapping against her cheeks. As he pushed into her, harder and harder, she cried out and rewarded him with a release of her sweet cream. Her hot moisture must have felt exquisite to him; so delicious that his own orgasm erupted, spewing hot jets into her. After withdrawing, he again sat in his chair, pulling her onto his lap.

John rested his head on her back, hugging her tightly. Jasmine remained sitting on her husband's lap with her eyes closed, taking in the sensations where her skin touched his. She fantasized that it was Patrick's lap she sat on, and Patrick's arms that were wrapped around her; she also imagined that it was he who was erect inside of her as they breathed each other in. She didn't mind the substitute at the moment, and thought that John didn't either, as he was likely longing for Morgan. After the sex they had just enjoyed, Jasmine found herself more desperate than ever to be with the one she truly loved. John sighed against her, mirroring the sentiment.

****

Later, as the family dined together, John and Jasmine were relaxed around each other for the first time in a long while. Brunne watched them, looking confused and slightly concerned. When there was a break in conversation, she suddenly announced, "Patrick called me today." Her words silenced the joyful chatter around the table, and Jasmine watched her intently, awaiting any information she would share.

John impatiently cleared his throat and urged, "Don't keep us all waiting, Ma. What did my little brother have to say?" He glared at Jasmine for a split second before looking back to his mother.

Taking her cue, Brunne proudly informed the family, "He ha' decided to cut hi' trip short and is returning right away. He should be home sometime tomorrow e'ening." Jasmine took a swift breath, and John roughly set his glass on the table. Brunne had paused to gauge their reactions, but then continued. "When he called, he wanted to talk to ye," she stated, nodding at Jasmine. "But I couldna find ye, and he was in flight, so we kept losing the connection."

Taking a gulp of her wine, Jasmine worked to regain her composure; she didn't want to seem too eager in front of her husband and mother-in-law. After taking a deep breath, she nonchalantly inquired, "He wanted to talk to me? Did he say what he needed?"

Glimpsing John's expression, she could see that he was confused, but she didn't dwell on him; it was Brunne she had to fool. When she looked at her mother-in-law, she could tell that the old lady was confused as well. *Does she know?* she wondered, her heart pounding. She studied the face of the mother of both her husband and the man she so deeply loved.

After a tense moment, Brunne finally said, "He didna say. He jus' asked how ye was a doin' and kept saying he couldna wait to be here and begin his life with his family." Jasmine sipped her wine as Brunne finished, and almost choked as she took in the words. She couldn't keep herself from looking at Callie at the mention of the word 'family'.

When she looked up, she realized that John had noticed and begun studying the child's face. Suddenly, he stood, knocking over his glass, and demanded, "I need to talk to you in my office. Now!" as he headed toward his destination.

On shaky legs, Jasmine followed her husband. As she pushed the office door open, her heart was beating wildly and she noticed that her hands were trembling.

When she entered his study, he was already pacing, wearing a path into the herringbone. "'Tis true?" he demanded in his accent that thickened when he was impassioned.

She took a deep breath, needing to sit on the sofa and collect her thoughts before she could answer him. "It may be true. I could not tell you without one of those- what the Americans call paternity tests. I learned about them on Maury."

Though her words were laced with humor in an attempt to calm him, John's anger continued to boil; he was impassive, and Jasmine's nervousness grew. He had never struck her, but learning that another man had fathered his child could be the last straw that pushed him over the edge.

She waited tensely for his reaction. He paced more frantically, and her nerves wound more and more tightly in response. "I know this must be difficult news for you to hear, my husband, and I only began considering it recently myself." Her words were meant to soothe him, but failed greatly, and he began running his hands through his hair: a sure sign of agitation.

"I promise you John, I didn't think of it until just today." When she saw that nothing she said would cool his anger, she volunteered, "Can I call for Morgan to come? She seems to be so good at calming you."

His pacing ceased abruptly, and he turned to her, considering her offer. In his heightened emotional state, his intense stare made her uncomfortable. When he didn't object, she found her phone in her pocket and pulled it out. "I will text her," she proposed.

When he did not move to prevent her, she began to punch in the message. After typing a few words, he stopped her, placing his hand over the screen. "Do not text her. Call her," he commanded. With quivering hands, Jasmine put the phone to her ear after pushing the call button, and then waited tensely.

Luckily, after the second ring, Morgan picked up. When Jasmine hesitated, Morgan asked, "Jasmine, is that you?"

Finding her voice finally, she sputtered, "Yes, it is me. I was wondering…that is…can you please come over? John…I mean we…need you here. I know it is very sudden, but could you please come now and help?"

Morgan was silent for a moment, but then responded, "Is everything okay, Jasmine? Of course. I can be there shortly. But what's going on?"

Jasmine took a deep breath before answering. Looking shyly at John while speaking into the phone, she admitted, "John is very upset. It is my fault. We just discovered…that is…John and I just realized that Callie may not be his child. We think she is Patrick's."

The phone was silent for a moment as the words were processed, and then Morgan said quietly, "I'm on my way. I'll be there shortly."

Jasmine passed the message on to her husband, and they stared silently at each other. Finally, he asked her to take the children and his mother somewhere; he had been dealt a blow, and needed some time to deal with it. Jasmine gladly complied, and left John alone in quiet solitude.

****

At OU Medical Center in the Neurology ICU, Morgan was getting restless. It was no surprise though, as she had been there all day. Luckily, she didn't receive the phone call from Jasmine until after Mag's family had arrived. Seeing that her best friend was surrounded by support and loved ones made it easier for Morgan to say her goodbyes and leave. But not before she pulled Maggie to the side and spoke with her, making sure that she would be okay.

"I have everything I need right now," she assured her. "Go. I know your number if I need you, and believe me, I *will* use it."

In her car, Morgan went over the situation in her mind. Jasmine had been in love with Patrick for some time. She thought that Callie, around two years in age, was Patrick's child. She and John had purchased the house four years ago, which meant that

Patrick and Jasmine had been together at some point after.

Morgan found this very curious; every time she'd seen John and Jasmine together, they had seemed madly in love. Even after buying the house, when she had spoken with them at Christmas parties thrown by her boss, they had seemed happily inseparable.

But then she considered the last Christmas party they had attended. Mack had chosen to host the black tie affair at the club house in Oak Tree. She recalled that the two had seemed loving to each other when they were close, but they had spent most of the party separate. Finishing her calculations, she decided that John must have discovered the affair shortly before that party. The couple had contacted her soon thereafter.

And considering the things John did to her, his sexuality was hyperactive; she couldn't imagine him going for any duration without satisfying those needs. *Talk about male whore*, she thought, with a smirk that had her blushing, as she drove toward her destination.

****

Arriving in John's driveway, Morgan's knees were weak already. She didn't know how he could have that effect on her- she was still angry from that morning– but she shook the thought off and went to the home's massive entrance. Before she could ring the bell, the oversized door opened. John stood just inside, a towel wrapped around his waist. He'd obviously just stepped out of the shower; his hair was still wet, and the scent of his moss soap wafted to her nose. It brought to mind the delicious things they had done together.

"You came," he observed, as he stepped out of the way for her to enter. Once inside, she stayed in the entryway, waiting for him to lead her to where he wanted to talk. When the door closed behind her with a loud thud, she turned to look at him.

Immediately, she became moist, and her legs weakened. She both hated and loved that he had that effect on her, but knew it couldn't be helped. Especially not when he watched her with his dark, hungry eyes; and certainly not when she could see his erection growing.

"I wanted to help, and it sounded as though you needed me." Not wanting to provoke his ire, she avoided mentioning his wife. As she spoke the words, she sounded breathless even to her own ears.

He noticed and moved to capture her. When he sensed no resistance, he pulled her into his arms. "I am so very thankful that you came," he whispered in her ear, accentuating the last word with a nip of her earlobe. She allowed herself to get lost for a moment in his embrace.

But then she pushed at his chest, creating a space between them. "I am happy to help in any way that I can," she stated sincerely. Looking him in the eye, she quietly asked, "How are you? It must have come as a horrible blow, and I'm sorry; it had to be incredibly hurtful."

His eyes went from hot and aroused to sorrowful at the mention of the source of his distress and sadness. She couldn't help but reach out to touch him, and then she pulled him in for an embrace. He hugged her so tightly that she thought she felt her ribs crack.

Afterwards, she looked up at him and stated, "You know it doesn't change anything."

He studied her for a moment, and then replied, "How can it not? It is a betrayal on a scale that I cannot even comprehend."

Morgan processed his words and then answered, "There was betrayal here. I agree with you on that. But where the child is concerned, it changes nothing. She has grown up knowing you as her father. You *are* still her father; do not punish her for her mother's sins. And from talking to Jasmine..." she trailed off, working to articulate the meanings of her thoughts. "I believe her when she says that she did not know. I don't think she was trying to hide it from you. I just believe that she has been thinking more about him lately, and it made her realize. I don't believe this was something she did on purpose."

They were both silent for a moment until she added, "The heart wants what it wants. The mind can fight it and try to reason with it, but in the end, it almost always wins. Besides, you can't help who you like or who you fall in love with."

As she reasoned with him, he began to see the wisdom in her words. "You are so smart, my judicious little one," he acknowledged, as he pulled her in for another intimate embrace. "See, I need you around so that you can keep me in check."

She did not pull away, so John kissed her forehead, and then moved his lips down her face before settling his lips on hers. "You let me kiss your beautiful face, my love. What else might you let me kiss?" he whispered huskily, as he rubbed his face on her neck.

Morgan allowed herself to get lost in his touches for a moment, but then she pushed him away. "I am not here for that," she said, poking her finger into his chest to accentuate each word. "I am here to help you through your difficulty."

She did very poorly at following through, however; while she was speaking, he pulled her into his erection and then kissed her deeply, to which she was very receptive. Before long, she wrapped her legs around him, and was carried swiftly to his office.

Once they arrived, he set her on the couch and then leaned down to capture her mouth with his. Soon he pulled her shirt up, baring her breasts for his inspection. When he brought his mouth toward her nipple, she arched her back, bringing it closer to him. He rewarded her with a quick nip, followed by a swipe of his tongue. "Mmmmm," she moaned, as her hips started to buck into his.

"Lift up for me," he commanded. "I want to see you naked and open for me." As he removed her pants, her hands went to his waist, and she ripped the towel away from him.

Free of barriers, his hands moved down her hips, holding her still for him. "I must taste you, my sweet," he said, as he pulled her to his mouth. Already wet for her lover, she was producing the sweet and tangy flavor that he ravenously devoured. Clamping himself to her as she moved into his mouth, he went to work, massaging her most sensitive spot.

He watched her face as he enjoyed her until he could hold back no longer. He moved up her body, his arousal impressive, as he pulled her hips forward, thrusting himself into her. Her cries of pleasure were all the answer he needed, and he continued to pound into her. "I want you so badly, my love," he exclaimed on an exhale, as he looked down at her through half-lidded eyes.

She smiled up at him and stroked his chest until she was so overcome by pleasure that she could do nothing but close her eyes to absorb all of the sensations. "Me too," she agreed, and as he kissed her, she moaned into his mouth, wanting everything he had to offer.

After thrusting into her several more times, they both came. He collapsed on top of her with his face buried in her neck, breathing in her smell. After a moment, he shifted his weight, causing her to groan as his movements sent a shiver of pleasure through her. Kneeling before her, he studied her face. She felt so relaxed and peaceful lying there, with him once again aroused and thick inside of her.

Finally he withdrew and then sat on the couch next to her. Her disappointment was obvious, but she smiled contentedly as he pulled her onto his lap. Skin to skin, and shoulder to chest, they sat, relaxing into each other while each gathered strength from the presence of the other.

"What would I have done if you hadn't come along?" he asked, stroking her face as he whispered intimately to her. She moved her cheek into his caresses, enjoying his sensuous touches.

After a moment, she answered him teasingly, "You would have rubbed a hole in your palm and owned stock in KY Jelly, I suspect." Despite all of the recent stresses, and how tightly wound he had become, he laughed at her statement.

After his chuckling subsided, he looked at her face and said, "You are right, my dear, but this is so much more delicious and fun." Placing his hand between her thighs, he added, "Plus it would be criminal to let this go to waste."

She purred at him. "I think you're right," she agreed, as she moved against his fingertips. She then admitted, "If not for you, I would've probably turned into an old cat lady; I didn't want anyone anywhere near me." She looked up at him as she finished her statement. "But there is just something about you that I can't get enough of, and the way you touch me…it has never been so…incredible. I have never had someone so tuned in to me. I feel like your body listens to my body, and then gives my body exactly what it wants and needs." She finished the last part of her statement as she grinded her bottom into his lap.

He responded, turned on by her antics. The way she moved against him caused him to become fully erect again. Placing his hands on her hips, he lifted her up and shared his fantasy, "I want to take you from behind and I want you bent over my desk while I do it."

She looked across the room at his desk and remembered her first time there when he and Jasmine had made love while watching her. The idea of him entering her in the same place caused her to become dampened, and she moved toward his desk. He remained seated as she grabbed the desk and bent herself over it, pushing out her bottom to entice him. He accepted the challenge, and moved to step up behind her.

Once he arrived at his destination, John clasped Morgan's hips and pulled her against him. It was not enough to have her merely next to him skin to skin; he wanted to taste her while he entered her. While she posed in front of him, he surveyed her, and then took her into his mouth, biting her shoulder. The marks he had recently put on her had yet to fade completely, and he was evidently satisfied as he continued to preserve them.

After biting down, he swiped the brand with his tongue, causing her to moan and push herself against him. He consequentially impaled her with his shaft, causing them both to cry out. Following her non-verbal cues, he remained inside her, thrusting over and over again. She continued to push against him as he pistoned into her. It didn't take long for him to have her moaning, and then she cried out his name, finally collapsing onto his desk, unable to hold herself up any longer.

Unfinished, he turned her over and entered her once more. Watching her breasts bounce to the force he created, he continued, the sound of his nuts slapping against her quite audible. As he thrust into her, she grasped his hand and suckled his middle finger, pulling it into her mouth. His breath caught as Morgan worked his extremity with her tongue; when she removed his finger from her mouth and placed it on her nipple, his struggle to hold back his orgasm was evident.

John closed his eyes, attempting to concentrate as he experienced only the delicious sensations that she provided. However, soon even that was too much for him, and gloriously he came, filling her. Looking to relieve her from the hard surface of his desk, he picked her up and brought her to the couch, spreading her body out to rest on top of him

"I have missed you so badly, my love, and it will not do to be apart from you," he told her as he looked down at her.

As he made this statement, the realization dawned on Morgan that she had not stood her ground and stayed away from him. "I've missed you too, John, but I still cannot move in with you." She said this as she laid back and worked to regulate her breathing.

As she lay across his chest, John studied her profile. Morgan knew that he was thinking about her last statement. She understood that, with her, he felt like he was home. He wanted to keep her close to him and protected; yet, he surely had to concede that, while perhaps not having her wholly at the present moment, having her in some capacity was better than losing her forever.

He took a deep breath and then announced, "I understand my love, and I cannot be without you." She opened her eyes and stared at him, trying to comprehend what he was saying. He nodded and acknowledged, "Yes, my love, I am saying I was wrong…in a way. I really would love for you to live here with me so that I can protect you, but it is not a requirement for our relationship." He waited a moment, watching the expressions chase across her face. "However, please do what I ask. I beg ye." he pleaded in his thickening Irish accent. "Please." He entreated her, "Do what I ask of ye, *mo shearc.*"

She blinked a few times and then focused on him. "But tell me what you are asking of me John," she requested.

"Allow me to send someone with ye to watch over ya."

She considered it for a moment and tried to imagine her life with a body guard. "I will put some thought into it," she told him. As a deep peace settled into their bones, they snuggled together, he kissing her on the head, and she kissing his chest.

Chapter Five

Patrick and Shannon were awakened during their trans-Atlantic flight to the sound of the captain speaking. Once alert, Shannon realized that they were being watched and tried to make sense of it. "That bloke is watching us, waiting for one of us to do something dodgy," Shannon announced.

"No way, mate," Patrick answered, obviously not believing his old friend. Shannon knew otherwise, as the man– pretending to casually observe them– continued to stare in their direction.

"Okay, ye can decide what ye'll choose ter believe, but right now I'm telling ye that we are being watched." He decided that the unusual attention was probably from all of their raucous behavior earlier in the flight. In all fairness, he thought with a smile, the wee lass who had served them their drinks had asked them several times to quiet down about halfway through the flight. He then considered that they had already been quite sloshed before boarding the plane, and the dozen– *or two*, his logical brain added– mini-bottles of whiskey likely hadn't helped.

Shannon's suspicions were confirmed when, upon arriving in New York City, the two men were escorted off the plane by airport security, driven away from the airport, and then deposited at a nearby convenience store.

****

Upon arriving at the small shop near the airport, the first thing Patrick did was call Jasmine. Luckily, she answered right away. "It's so good to hear your voice, my beloved," he told her.

"Patrick! Where are you? Your mother said you were coming back already." He had hoped his mother had passed along the news, but wondered how his older brother felt about it. As if she could read his mind she informed him, "John is okay with us, Patrick." The way she said it... *It sounds like she means that John is allowing us to be together permanently,* he thought. But, that couldn't possibly be true.

When he didn't respond to her news, she prompted, "Have you changed your mind about us, Patrick?"

He could hear the tears beginning to gather in her voice and hurried to reassure her. "I could never change the way I feel about ye, even if I tried, Jasmine. And believe me, I've tried." Her relief was palpable even over the phone, and he could hear her letting out her breath. "What do ye mean he is okay wi' us?" he asked her.

She explained, "I mean he wants us to be together. He has found someone that he is madly in love with, and he is okay with you and I being together."

"Wha'…you mean…" He was speechless for a moment, unable to believe his fortune. Jasmine was silent, giving him time to absorb the information. Finally, he said, "My love, ye're words are unbelievable, and I…I am speechless. We can really be together withou' pretendin' or sneakin'?"

Excitedly, she explained that John had finally decided that he could not move past her infidelity. She also confirmed that upon Patrick's return they would be free to begin their relationship together anew. He absorbed the information for a moment before remembering his travel predicament. Disbelieving the irony of their situation, Patrick growled while shaking his head and began to tell her of his tale.

"You won' floggin' believe this, me love." He slapped his own forehead as he recounted the events from the flight. After he summarized his circumstances, he exclaimed, "And now I've been kicked from the airport and missed my connecting flight! How is it that ye are finally mine after all this time, an' because I became so bloody sloshed I canna have ye just yet; what with you half the country away an' all?"

Initially, her silence suggested she was saddened by the delay, likely feeling bad for her lover's misfortune. Then she blurted out an idea that sparked new excitement and elicited relief. "I'll come get you!" she exclaimed. "It'll be a fun little road trip. I'll bring your mother and the girls, and it'll give John time alone with Morgan." She hesitated for a moment, and then explained about his brother's new lover.

After discussing the route, the two decided that Patrick would rent a car, and they would meet in Indianapolis. Patrick and Jasmine hung up, and he went to work locating a rental agency.

****

Jasmine felt giddy. To her surprise, Brunne was not only accepting, but she actually seemed happy that they were going to pick up Patrick. Jasmine thought she must be imagining it, but the old woman actually seemed happy about the prospect of Jasmine's and Patrick's relationship. She had not yet disclosed her plans to Brunne, but somehow the old lady knew, as she told Jasmine that she would make Patrick very happy.

Feeling elated, Jasmine began packing and preparing for the road trip. It would be a long one with two small children, but at least she would be travelling at night, and the girls would be asleep.

After getting herself and her children packed, she went into John's office to let him know the details of the plan. Shockingly, she walked right in on her husband and Morgan making love. John was sitting on the couch with Morgan's mouth enveloping his shaft in an erotic, throaty dance. Jasmine watched for a moment, and couldn't believe how turned on she was becoming.

She was caught off guard, but thought they would notice her and stop. However, John's head was back, and the look on his face told her that he was too caught up in the moment to notice her, while Morgan was busy with him in her mouth. Jasmine pondered her husband's size and couldn't understand how Morgan could take all of him inside of her like that; in all of their time together, she had never been able to take it all, and in fact it often hurt when he was inside of her down below.

After watching them for a while, she noticed the damp heat pooling between her thighs. It must have been like this for Morgan that first time when she had watched John and Jasmine together. Finally, John's fists gripped her hair and he slammed into her while yelling out, "Fuck, Morgan! Your mouth is so hot!" She surmised that he must have orgasmed then, because Morgan finally released him and climbed into his lap.

After snuggling her head into his shoulder, Morgan looked over and noticed Jasmine for the first time. "Jasmine, hi," she said shyly, as she used John's arms to cover herself. Jasmine couldn't help but smile at Morgan's bashfulness. John's reaction was typical: he smiled at her arrogantly and groped himself while looking at her salaciously.

Jasmine was still turned on by the show she had just seen. Though she typically didn't care for his arrogance, it was adding fuel to the fire in her heightened state of arousal. She had to clear her throat before she could address the couple, but then stated, "I came to let you know… something." She trailed off, momentarily forgetting all reason and needing to collect herself.

John was stroking Morgan's nipples, as well as between her legs where his hand covered her. Every so often, he would switch breasts so that Morgan was exposed to the room. Jasmine was immensely aroused by her nakedness and by watching John work her body. Morgan's moans didn't help, and Jasmine found herself wanting to join them. Strange, she thought, how even though the roles were reversed, she still found it incredibly hot.

"Shall I come back?" she asked in a hoarse voice that was nearly a whisper.

While she awaited an answer, John's massage of the throbbing and slick nerve bundle at the junction of Morgan's inner thighs became more vigorous, and he whispered something in her ear that was followed with a nibble. Her swift intake of breath told Jasmine that John was doing what he was really good at: touching his lover in the way he knew to be the most pleasurable for her.

She watched his rhythmic jerky movements for a moment until her thoughts were cut off. He released Morgan of his hold down below and crooked his finger at Jasmine, beckoning for her to join them and exposing Morgan's slick core to the room.

Her legs moved of their own volition as they carried her to the duo on the couch. John guided her to sit on his thigh that was not occupied by Morgan, and she complied. As he brought his fingers that had occupied Morgan's vagina to his nose and sniffed, Jasmine looked at the other woman through half-lidded eyes…and then captured her mouth.

After the sultry kiss, Jasmine glanced briefly at her husband before telling Morgan, their shared lover, "I have wanted you so badly. I've missed this." She placed her fingers on Morgan's heated entrance that John's fingers had so recently occupied. The answering moan was the assurance Jasmine needed, and she moved toward an exposed breast, stroking her nipples with her tongue while pushing John out of the way.

Interestingly, as Jasmine took more of Morgan's breast into her mouth, John's tension grew, though Jasmine was beyond the point of worrying over his concerns. Soon she prompted Morgan to lie on her back. Jasmine made her way down Morgan's body with her mouth, from breast to belly to delicate pubic skin. She buried her face there, her exposed lover draped over John's thighs. Morgan's moans told her that she was in the right spot, and she increased the pressure.

John watched the show and eventually began to stroke himself. Once Jasmine had her face buried in Morgan, John placed his hand on Jasmine's bottom, moving it downward. He hovered over the entryway to her most sacred cavum. She lifted her head, momentarily unable to continue her tongue massage, as she felt his presence there. She turned her head to look at him, questioning his intentions and his reasons for intimately touching her.

While John remained still, Morgan frantically thrust herself against Jasmine's chin. Jasmine brought her mouth back to Morgan's core and again took her wholly into her mouth. As she did this, John entered his wife with his fingers and sensuously massaged her in that skilled way of his. As much as Jasmine wanted to complain, she was too caught up in the moment.

She caressed with her tongue, and Morgan responded with bucking hips and breathy moans. Jasmine lost herself in the sensations until she noticed her own ragged breathing, aroused from the pleasure of John's fingers. As she mouthed Morgan, John brought his own mouth to his wife and swirled his tongue persistently. She called out, so enticed by his sensuous massage. Jasmine continued to caress Morgan until she lost all control and exploded in her mouth.

Jasmine tried to ignore the constant pressure that John inflicted upon her, massaging the place he knew to be her most tender, sensitive spot. She didn't want to be affected by him, but he worked her body like a musical instrument of which he had intimate knowledge. She couldn't stop her uncontrollable impulses, and she couldn't prevent her hips from bucking against his tongue. As she moved up Morgan's body so that she could kiss her lips and retreat from her husband's sensual assault, John remained affixed to her.

Morgan lay back with her eyes closed in her post-cunnilingus bliss and allowed Jasmine's mouth full access to her body. Jasmine took advantage of this invitation and responded with her lips, suckling Morgan's breasts occasionally and licking unceasingly while she softly twisted her lover's nipples in her fingertips. After a moment of listening to Morgan's keening moans, Jasmine's hand descended and she swirled a massage over her lover's already throbbing nub.

As she devoured the lover she'd once shared with her husband, John became more aggressive with his finger work. Jasmine wanted to resist the effect he had on her body; in an attempt to distract herself, she replaced her mouth on Morgan's core, where she resumed her craft, eliciting ever-louder moans.

While she tasted and enjoyed and performed her own massage of Morgan's clit, John continually dipped his fingers deep into his wife, caressing the spot that he knew gave her the most pleasure. She moaned around Morgan's skin as her lover moaned in response to what she was doing.

Jasmine wanted so much to give Morgan pleasure, but she lost her concentration when John again placed his mouth where his fingers had been. Unable to move, she froze, her lips affixed to Morgan's breast and her fingers just inside of Morgan's satin sheath.

Jasmine lifted her face for a breathless moment, unable to see or feel anything other than John's mouth meting out pleasure. After a moment, Morgan gripped her shoulders, prompting her to return and finish her work. As her dark-haired lover moaned, directing her, John's tongue probed Jasmine hungrily, causing her to move against his welcoming orifice. As he devoured her, she in turn massaged her lover until finally they both orgasmed, Morgan with a moan into Jasmine's mouth, and Jasmine into her husband's mouth. Both women then collapsed, breathless together.

Fully satisfied with what had transpired, John grinned and kissed both of their foreheads as he pulled them both close to him. The two women drew near to each other, kissing and embracing as they pulled each other onto John's lap.

"You are so generous, my lover," Jasmine whispered to Morgan.

Morgan looked confused for a moment. Then, realization seemed to dawn as she grasped Jasmine's meaning: *You are generous in the way you share my husband.* With a quick laugh, Morgan protested, "No, let's get this straight. You are the generous one. I would be nowhere if not for your unselfish sharing of your husband. This could not have happened without your willingness to allow me to have him." Morgan continued to explain her feelings as John rubbed her shoulders with one hand and embraced his wife with the other.

Jasmine considered her words as she absorbed the feeling of her husband's touch. Finally, she responded, "Yes, I agree, but he would not have allowed it had you not been here to feed his nymphomaniac appetite."

John pulled her hair lightly at this comment, causing her to cry out, and Morgan's eyes widened. Capturing his hand, she suckled his fingertips and said, "You are correct in your observation of his…," she had to clear her throat before she could complete the statement, but then smiled and finished, "mythical appetite." She stared into John's eyes. "But that's perfect, because I am starving for what he has to give me." She pointedly stroked him and then kissed his lips.

John had watched her intently while she worked his hand with her mouth, and now he pulled her more snuggly against his body. "I agree. I cannot help myself when you are around," he stated as he kissed her on the mouth.

Jasmine watched them and felt a brief twinge of regret that she had given up John and his passion. The thought made her long for Patrick that much more. That longing quickly dissipated, however, when she thought of the love and passion she felt for Patrick, and that she would soon be with him. She suddenly pushed herself up and off of John's lap.

When they both looked at her in inquiry, she explained, "I must go. Patrick is driving in a rental.

The girls and your mom and I are going to meet him halfway."

Morgan expressed her excitement by clapping her hands. Standing, she kissed Jasmine on the mouth and exclaimed, "I'm so happy for you, Jasmine! You deserve this!"

Jasmine was taken aback, but was excited all the same. She kissed Morgan on the lips, and then John on the forehead, and said her goodbyes.

After Jasmine left, Morgan settled back onto John's lap. Kissing him, she exclaimed, "Wow! That was hot." She hesitated briefly, and then started, "John, are you sure?"

Sensing her insecurity, he prompted, "What, *mo shearc*? You can ask me anything."

Before continuing, Morgan gathered her confidence in order to articulate her thoughts. Finally, she said, "Are you sure you two are making the right decision? I mean, I know things have happened between you, but watching the two of you together just now..." He waited patiently for her to continue. "I can see some great chemistry between the two of you. I just want you to be sure about this before you continue with me...and before either of you do something you can't take back."

John was silent for a moment, as if considering her statements. Then, he emphatically answered, "Listen to me in this and know that I tell the truth, my love. Jasmine and I are finished. We have been finished for a very long time now. Even before I knew that she and Patrick were intimate, I knew that she was not in love with me. It was likely in the way that we met. I saw her while she was in a bad way, and some people never come back from that. Every time she looked into my eyes, I think she was reminded of that time; while with me, she could never see herself as more."

He spoke to her softly as he caressed her lips with his thumb. "I think it is like this with her. In a sense, I rescued her from her fate. When she and I first met, she seemed very intimidated by me. I was very much in love with her, but I have a very dominant personality. She was so fragile, and she still remains so in many ways. I think she felt she had to do everything I asked of her…and she did, even when she didn't want to. I didn't realize this at first. But looking back, I can see that it was so."

He took a deep breath and let it out. The regret was clearly visible on his face as he explained, "I wish I had known what was happening at the time. I could have been gentler with her. But in all actuality, I am who I am…and she is who she is. There is no changing that, and I don't think anything could have changed our fate."

Morgan watched him as he explained, feeling sadness for both him and Jasmine. Even so, a sense of relief filled her; she was happy that he had no reservations. Further, she was glad that his wife was free to explore her love interest. Kissing him on the cheek, Morgan told him, "I am so happy for us, Love. And for Jasmine."

His brow furrowed at the mention of his wife's name, and Morgan raised her hand to smooth his forehead. "Now now, dear…you can't scowl every time her name is mentioned. It won't do. She is the mother of your children, and will continue to be part of your family for a very long time."

John's dark expression cleared as he said, "Alas, you are right, my little flower. I did not realize that I was scowling. I will keep that in mind for future reference." Morgan was sitting so close to him; so accessible that he was unable to resist the urge to kiss her. After sucking her lips into his mouth, he released her and held her closely.

"My dear one, I need to ask you something that I have wondered about," he said quietly. Morgan looked up at him wide-eyed, wondering what could cause him to be so curious and so nervous; in her experience, John was rarely one to be unsure of himself. But then, he asked a question which had obviously been on his mind for a while. "Could you tell me why you are so insistent about not moving in with me?" He looked deeply into her eyes, awaiting an answer.

Morgan maintained eye contact with him and answered simply, "Yes. My children are the biggest reason. They have been in the same school district for years. My oldest two children are in high school, and it's already hard enough without the upheaval of changing schools in the middle of the year."

John stared at her intently, considering her words. After a moment, she continued, "The other reason is that it's too soon, John. I'm a single mom, and first and foremost I must consider my children. I wouldn't think about moving in with a man that I had only just begun to date. I want to get to know you better before I introduce you to them. I also want to make sure you are going to be good with them before considering such a big step. What if you hate each other?"

John was silent for a moment, but then conceded, "Okay, that makes sense. Can I at least meet your children, so that we can get the ball rolling? I don't know that seeing you only sparsely will be enough for me."

Morgan had to laugh, which prompted John to pinch her still-bared nipple. He asked, "What is so funny, my little vixen?"

In retaliation, she bit the fingers that had just pinched her. "You have a whorish appetite, Mr. Kennedy; not just a nympho one," she teased, as he pulled his hand back.

He tried to keep a straight face, but his smile broke through, causing him to shed ten years. "Just for that, I will have to punish you," he announced. He then turned her over so that her bottom was perched over his lap. She feigned resistance for a moment, but soon he brought his hand down and smacked her cheek, which he followed with a bite and then a lick, causing her to moan.

"I have been a very naughty girl, sir," she announced, turning her head to look over her shoulder at him.

"Is that so, young lady?" he asked with a wolfish grin. She lifted her bottom slightly in answer, ready for more of his delicious 'punishment'. He did not disappoint her.

He slapped her other cheek, and once again his mouth was on her, providing the same biting and licking attention. She wondered how many times she would get to feel him; however, her thoughts were cut off by his fingers entering her feminine channel, and she gasped for breath. As he twisted his fingers, she could only moan, trying to move enough air into her lungs. His touch was building an exquisite pressure within her. While increasing the force of his fingers down below, he slapped her cheek once more, eliciting another moan.

"You are so wet for me, Morgan. I want to punish you more, but I must taste you." After he breathed this to her, his mouth was on her; on the place where his fingers were dancing so intimately.

She cried out as his tongue entered her, and he made quick work of coaxing her to a raging orgasm once again. She grabbed his head and cried out, pleading for him to enter her.

Smiling, he looked down at her and refused. "This is part of your punishment, dear. You will have to learn to accept your consequences." He continued to move his tongue in and out of her.

Morgan's head tossed back and forth frantically on the pillow in a vain effort to dispel some of the building pressure. Finally, she cried out, "John, please! I need you inside me! Now!" This had worked in the past, and she hoped her plea would serve the same purpose once again. However, he continued to taunt her with his mouth while she writhed with pleasure that bordered on pain.

"That will not work for you this time, my little playboy," John's muffled voice said, his mouth still on her. "I want to watch your face and know that you are needing me as badly as I am needing you."

Her head continued to thrash, and he took pleasure in the knowledge that he was inflicting such strong sensations within her.

Finally, he stopped and moved to the floor, kneeling, and staring down at her. Morgan's eyes were wild, awaiting his entry. She stared at him, entreating him without making a sound. Suddenly grabbing her hips, he buried himself inside her, causing her to moan loudly. He took her with force, building the fire for both of them.

She had already had several orgasms by this point; but with John's powerful penetration, this one was much stronger and much more satisfying. Her orgasm built to an all-consuming force that ripped through her, leaving her completely sated and relaxed. As the overwhelming intensity of her orgasm subsided, John reached his own orgasm, yelling out her name and collapsing on top of her. They looked at one another, covered in sweat and spent from their recent strenuous activities.

After calming from the storm of sensations, Morgan felt chilled, and a small shiver overtook her. John reached to grab a blanket, covering them both. Snuggling for the night, they fell asleep together for a second night, skin to skin and wrapped in each other's arms. Morgan couldn't remember any time that she felt happier or more fulfilled.

Chapter Six

Maggie checked her watch for the fifth time that hour, disappointed to see that it was only 9:30 p.m. She felt a terrible sense of dread since her grandmother was on the way; the same grandmother that hadn't taken the time to see her daughter since learning about her diagnosis three years earlier.

As much as she wanted to keep the peace, Mag wasn't sure that she would be able to refrain from saying nasty words to her. She had listened to her mother cry herself to sleep on numerous occasions- often after an attempt to call the old bat- and Maggie had plenty of anger built up against the wicked old shrew. Luckily, Pete was there and could handle their grandma; as timid as he'd once been, he was much closer to the old lady and was willing to stand up to her when necessary.

She had studied the pattern of the linoleum in her mother's room for five more hours before the dreaded appearance was made manifest. Unfortunately, Pete was nowhere to be seen and Maggie was alone in the ICU bay. After looking up to see her enter, she pointedly stared at the floor and decided it was better to ignore her than to say something she could not take back, or to disturb her mother's death slumber; and she certainly was not going to leave her mother alone with the old crone.

Her thoughts were cut off by the clearing of a throat, and Maggie reluctantly looked up to see her grandmother staring down at her expectantly. The incensed look on the gnarled face was nearly enough to make Maggie see red, but she managed to keep her mouth shut and her temper in check. When the two women continued to stare, the old biddy rudely demanded, "If you'll excuse me, I would like a few moments alone with my daughter."

Maggie thought back to when she was much younger and very intimidated by her grandmother. The old woman would lock her and Pete in the attic, and sometimes pull or cut her hair if she was extremely displeased- and that was just the cruelties she could remember. Thinking back to the terror she had experienced at the old lady's hands fueled her anger toward the woman who stood indignantly, demanding that she leave.

Despite her boiling fury, Maggie responded in a quiet but adamant voice. "I will do no such thing. You lost that privilege when you abandoned your daughter at the worst possible time. And if you don't like it you can go to hell."

The old lady's eyes widened, and she lifted her hand as if to strike Maggie. Mag stood her ground and awaited the blow, refusing to blink or look away. With lightning speed that seemed supernatural for a seemingly frail elderly woman, the blow landed, leaving in its wake a searing pain.

They both remained upright, staring daggers at each other. Neither dared to look away. To the ignorant onlooker, they would likely have appeared a timeless duo- a battle of wills that could have originated centuries earlier.

The smoldering pain on Maggie's cheek faded into nothingness as she stared down her grandmother. She had cowered for so long, gripped by the fear that had been her constant companion– fear of *this woman.* She decided at this moment that it would go on no longer. She stood her ground, refusing to acknowledge pain or self-doubt. As she breathed deeply and deliberately, she felt herself somehow grow taller until she nearly towered over the ancient creature before her.

Finally, a change took place in the old lady- an internal battle only clear to those who knew her most intimately. After years of suffering abuse from this woman, Maggie was one of the few who possessed this deeper knowledge of the monster she faced down; she continued to stand her ground.

Following this unspoken but epic battle of wills, the elderly woman finally lowered her eyes, understanding at last that she could no longer intimidate the 'girl-child'. She ducked her head and on her heel. Looking remarkably like a cowering animal, she left the room without saying another word.

Maggie somehow knew that this was the last time she would see her grandmother.

Throughout the night, Mag's mom had ups and downs. There were times when she didn't breathe for several moments before finally gasping for breath; then there were times when her O2 saturation decreased to the 70's but then improved spontaneously. Owing to her nursing experience, Maggie understood that her mother was in the final stages of death. Further, she could hear the death rattle emanating from her throat.

When her brother asked what was happening, she articulated in the best way she knew. She told him that death is not like it is shown in movies, explaining that it doesn't typically happen very quickly, and expressing to him that the body is an amazing thing that tries to find a way to live. Though her brother seemed impressed with her insight and knowledge, it did nothing to allay Maggie's feeling of pending doom.

****

Morgan's unexpected return, and her bright presence the next morning helped to lift Maggie's spirits. The underlying joy that emanated from Morgan caused Maggie to feel more at peace about her mother's pending death. It was in the way that even when Morgan wasn't smiling, she radiated happiness, rather than the gloom that had dominated Mag of late.

Not wanting to leave her mother's side, Mag directed her best friend to the two chairs in the nearby corner so that they could talk. Curious to hear more about Morgan's tumultuous romance, she asked, "So, what happened?"

The smile that came across Morgan's face could have illuminated the entire room, and Maggie's curiosity was further piqued; she knew it must have something to do with her new lover. "Spill it, girl. What's been happening?" Maggie prodded with a smile.

When Morgan started to deny the accusation, Maggie confronted her with an impassive expression. After a brief standoff, a volley of giggles burst from both women. Morgan quickly covered her mouth, feeling guilty about laughing in such a tragic setting. Rather than delivering a reprimand, Maggie surprised her by smiling herself and then giggling in response.

"He changed his mind!" Maggie suddenly exclaimed, reading the elation in her friend's eyes.

"He couldn't be without you!" Morgan's answering smile and blush was all the confirmation she needed. "Oh, my gosh! I'm so happy for you, Morgan. You deserve to be this happy in a relationship." After sharing a moment of quiet joy, she asked, "What's he like, and when do I get to meet him?"

Morgan looked hesitant, deliberating the question. Then, she appeared to make a decision. "Maybe tomorrow night? I'll check with John and see if he's available. That is…" She looked toward Maggie's mother, worry plainly evident on her face; she didn't want to be insensitive about her friend's impending loss.

Mag recognized her anxiety, and put her hand up to stop Morgan, reassuring, "No worries, friend. I'm going crazy here, and by tomorrow evening I will need a break." She left unspoken the fact that her mother was close to taking her last breath and likely wouldn't last that long.

"Okay," Morgan said, smiling, "we'll play it by ear. How are you holding up?"

Maggie put on her brave face– the same one she had been wearing around visiting family members– and replied, "I'm fine. I think that knowing this was going to happen has made it much easier on me."

Morgan stared at her for a moment and then gave her a speech very similar to the one she'd delivered the day before. "I call bullshit on that one, Mags. Just like you know when I'm lying, I can sense your fibs from miles away. So let's try this again. How are you holding up?"

Maggie knew that Morgan had seen through her façade, and there was no reason to keep up the charade with her BF. Dropping the act, Maggie hugged her, and then cried silently into her shoulder, accepting the support that Morgan had instinctively known was needed. They embraced for several minutes; finally Maggie lifted her head and wiped her eyes. "Thank you for that," she said to her friend, and that was all that was necessary for the time.

After sitting in companionable silence for some time, Mag suddenly remembered the telephone call she had received the previous evening. "Hey, your mom called me last night," she began. Morgan looked up, raising her eyebrows slightly. Maggie explained the offer from Morgan's mother to return early from Florida should support be needed at the hospital, stating, "I told her not to come back early for this, and explained that my mom doesn't need extra people sitting around to watch her pass; she's sleeping peacefully and is pain-free. Plus, with the kids coming back and Steve being gone, I think they should enjoy their vacay for as long as possible." With hardly a pause, Maggie asked, "What are you going to tell them anyways?"

Morgan's expression showed that she'd noticed the subtle change of subject, but obviously chose to ignore it. "I haven't decided yet, truthfully," she responded, "but I still have three days to figure it out. Oh yeah, I should probably call the detectives again." After an uncomfortable moment, she hesitantly asked, "Did my mom have anything else to talk to you about?"

She definitely saw the guilty expression that crossed Maggie's face; the air of suspicion in the room was palpable as Morgan waited for the withheld information. "What else did you tell my mom?" she asked, sounding alarmed. When Maggie hesitated, Morgan's anxiety seemed to skyrocket.

"I'm sorry, Morgan. My grief must have been talking because she…she bullied me, and you know I've almost always got your back. But she knew something was up because you hadn't called her in like two days."

Morgan bit her tongue and admitted, "Okay, that's my fault. What did you tell her?"

Mag took a deep breath before answering her friend. "I told her you seemed really happy and that I hadn't met him yet."

"What else?" Morgan persisted.

"I also told her that he has kids and an ex-wife, but that the two of you get along famously." Maggie said the last with a giggle; considering the participants, the relationship probably could be somewhat famous.

Morgan processed the information before asking, "Is that it?"

Mag's nod seemed to satisfy her best friend, but Morgan's lingering worries were evident as she silently sat pondering her situation: was she prepared to introduce John to her parents? Maggie was lost in thought over her friend's conundrum. Considering their passion that Morgan had described, would she and John be able to keep their hands off of each other during such an encounter? Maggie summoned a mental picture of Morgan jumping on John, his hands on her body, while her parents sat in shocked silence on the sofa. Shaking her head, she dismissed the ludicrous image; all the same, Morgan's mother would be chomping at the bit until she met her daughter's love interest, so Morgan would have to find a way to work it out.

Maggie's thoughts were interrupted when Dr Schambaugh entered and walked up to her.

"How are we doing today?" he asked.

Mag was happy to see him as she jumped up and met him halfway across the room. However, she answered him somberly, "I think mom is in the final stages, but she is resting peacefully and comfortably."

As the doctor approached her, rubbing her shoulder in apparent sympathy, she noticed Morgan's eyes narrowing in suspicion. Maggie didn't know the source of her friend's discomfort, but she obviously was put off by Dr. Schambaugh. Turning to look at him, she couldn't see anything in particular that could explain Morgan's reticence. His face *did* seem to take on an aristocratic, almost superior expression when he wasn't talking; but he had seemed so sincere when praising the quality of nursing care she had provided to her mother.

After a few minutes, Maggie thanked Dr. Schambaugh for his concern and walked him to the door of the room. As he departed, Morgan watched him closely. As soon as he was out of hearing range, her friend shared her observation. "There's something about that man that rubs me the wrong way."

Mag turned to her, confused, and said, "Really? I think he's kinda hot. And he's probably not a bad guy if he made it all the way into a fellowship. I'm actually looking forward to having lunch with him."

When Morgan glanced toward her, Maggie smiled, feeling happy for the first time in a long while. Her friend returned the smile, nodding to acknowledge that, where men were concerned, Mag should trust her own judgment. She thought that a friendship with the kind doctor might be good for her. However, Morgan's sly smile and faint chuckle spelled out her friend's thoughts clearly: *What Maggie needs is to get laid.*

****

After a few hours of staying at the hospital with Mag, the nursing staff came in and announced, "We're here to bathe Miss Sumner." Morgan and Maggie retreated to the hall outside, giving the nurses the room and privacy needed to do their jobs.

At some point during the sponge bath, the alarms sounded. Both women held their breath, awaiting news as the minutes passed with agonizing slowness. Finally, the nurses stepped out to inform Maggie that her mother had passed peacefully as she was being bathed. Morgan looked at her best friend and was surprised to see relief in her face as they walked back into the ICU bay.

"I'm thankful it happened this way," Mag told her in answer to her concerned expression. As none of her other family members were yet ready to join them around the corpse, Mag and Morgan were alone for the moment. Mag obviously sensed her confusion and explained, "When a person is close to death in situations like this, but they are hanging on, sometimes the staff will come in and bathe them. It serves to prepare the body so that there are no unwanted fluids hanging around that tend to come out of the body during the dying process."

Maggie looked around as if checking that they were still alone before continuing. "Also, when the patient is so close to dying, turning them on their left side uses gravity to shunt the fluids to the heart. Since the heart is already so close to ending its course within the body, the added stress overloads it and the person dies."

Morgan raised an eyebrow slightly, surprised at the clinical detachment with which Maggie was able to deliver her explanation. Noticing her bewilderment, Mag reaffirmed, "I told you, I'd already somewhat prepared myself for this. It's sad, but I knew it was close, and every day I had left with her was a gift." When Morgan continued to look concerned, Maggie added, "Seeing it this way helps me, Morg. Really: it's better that she went peacefully, and more humane that the nursing staff took care of it when she had just been given a dose of morphine. I'm honestly glad that my mother had such a dignified death."

Finally appeased, Morgan took a deep breath and asked what else needed to be done to help with arrangements.

"The chaplain has arranged everything that is needed at this point, in accordance with the plans my mom laid out last year," Maggie assured her. Then, as an afterthought, she said, "But go hug my brother, Morgan. Pete has always cared about you a great deal. Your presence will help him."

Morgan smiled and nodded, leaving to find Pete. A quick search found him sitting quietly in the waiting room, an unread magazine open on his lap. He looked both anxious and tired, and she knew by the apprehensive look he gave her that her message was not unexpected.

If Mag was a reserved crier, Pete was the opposite. Morgan held him as he wept loudly, racked by deep resounding sobs. After several moments, he stopped to blow his nose, and then asked her to accompany him to his mother's deathbed.

To Morgan's dissatisfaction, Dr. Schambaugh was in the room with Mag again, and they appeared to be conversing intimately. When the newcomers entered, he straightened, Maggie blushing faintly. The doctor then announced time of death to the group and left hastily.

"Eleven twenty-four," Maggie repeated. "That was my mom's birthday." Absent-mindedly, she hugged her brother, and then said she would be outside if anyone needed her.

After staying a while longer, Morgan decided that she needed to get some work done; she said her goodbyes, quickly visiting with each of Maggie's loved ones.

As she left, she texted John that she needed to go in to the office for a while, and that she would call when she was leaving. His answering text had her both smiling and blushing a deep red:

> I can't wait to see you when you get off work. Don't even consider not coming to see me tonight…I need your hot pussy ☺

An hour later, Morgan sat in her office ready to get some work done. Noting the day of the week, she was irritated that her ex-husband and McCrazy the stalker had caused her to lose several days' worth of productivity. She started the laborious task of returning phone calls and emails. By three o'clock she had finally tied up loose ends; all but one. She could ignore it no longer; it was time to call Detective Rice.

He picked up after the third ring. "Miss Freeman," he said without preamble. She was momentarily taken aback. *Must have known it was me by caller ID,* she thought sourly. *And probably does that to get people off guard.* She answered him nonchalantly, not wanting to give him the satisfaction. "Yes, it is Miss Freeman," she confirmed before inquiring about the status of her case.

After entertaining her queries, he had questions of his own; before she knew it, she had been on the phone with him for forty-five minutes. When he finally sounded like he was finished, she requested, "Can I ask one last thing?" After his affirmation, she said, "Steve's current wife has called me a couple of times. What should I tell her?"

The detective seemed baffled, as the line went silent for a while; so long, in fact, that she wondered if the connection had been lost. Finally, however, he instructed her, "I would like to have her notified via police. Don't answer her phone calls until we let her know. I will call you once that happens." As Morgan hung up the phone, she was relieved not to be tasked with the unpleasant job of death notification.

Noting the time, Morgan discovered that, even though she had worked only a half day, she was drained. She made a hasty exit, wishing to avoid her nosy co-workers, while sending her boss, Mack a cursory text notifying him that she was leaving for the day. When she finally sat in her car, she stopped to take a few deep breaths, decompressing while she inhaled the scent of her leather interior.

After collecting herself, she called her mother, wanting to check on her children. She was surprised at how happy she felt, and how calming she found their voices. Jennie's voice squeaked, she was so excited about Disney World, and Ben actually sounded excited as well, which was rare for him, enveloped as he was in his teenage flattened affect.

However, the one who surprised her most was Stacia, and it wasn't her enthusiasm. Ominously, the conversation began only after her oldest daughter removed herself to a room where she could not be overheard. Morgan was concerned; perhaps Stacia wasn't ignorant of Monday night's events…perhaps the media had tipped her off somehow about her murdered stepfather.

When Stacia started talking, there was something in her voice that told Morgan that she was frightened. "Have you talked to Lucia lately, Mom?" she asked, already sounding alarmed. When Morgan informed her that she hadn't, her daughter nearly became frantic, pleading with her mom to go check on her.

"What's this about, Stacia?" Morgan asked, wanting some insight into the source of her daughter's distress. She could hear breathing on the line as though her daughter was working to calm herself. Waiting patiently, Morgan knew that her daughter would talk when she was ready.

After what seemed like forever, the girl continued. "You know what it's like to see a friend starting down a bad path and so you try to stop them, but it's like there's nothing you can do but sit back and watch?"

Morgan had a bad feeling, anxious about what her daughter would reveal. "Yes, I've had the feeling," she confirmed. Before she could complete her affirmation, Stacia was talking on top of her.

"Well, I've had this feeling lately that she has been doing drugs, and I know her mom does stuff… drugs and stuff…like every day. So I've been paying closer attention to her, and I've been really worried about her. I don't think she's been to school at all this week, Mom, and I think whatever she's doing has become really bad. Will you please go check on her? She won't answer my phone calls."

Morgan considered her daughter's request before assuring her, "Yes, Stacia, I will go check on her right now. And hun…" She waited until she knew she had her daughter's attention before continuing. "I'm really proud of you for coming to me with this. I will do whatever I can to see that she is taken care of."

After saying her goodbyes, Morgan headed for the home of Lucia and her mother. When she pulled into their driveway, she noticed that the family car was in its usual spot. Approaching the front door, she rang the bell and waited…no answer. With a sinking feeling, she rang the doorbell repeatedly while also knocking on the door. Considering the fact that Miss Dean rarely left the home, Morgan was very concerned. After knocking once more, she tried the door knob, finding it unlocked.

Inside, the house smelled awful…as if something had died. Looking around, she saw trash and old food piled up on the floor. Walking through the hall, she came to Miss Dean's room first. The woman lay sprawled out on the bed. Morgan could see that she was breathing, so she left her and continued to Lucia's room.

What she found sickened her. The stench of urine permeated the room. Lucia was in a pool of her own dried vomit and it looked as though she had been there for several days. Morgan shook Lucia and yelled her name to try and arouse her. When she saw that the little girl would not be awakened, she pulled her phone from her pocket and dialed 911.

Dispatch asked her to check for a pulse. After verifying that one existed, they instructed her to clear the patient's airway and turn her on her side. Next they had her rub vigorously on her chest with her knuckles, which did not elicit a response. Morgan noted that where she felt the little girl's skin at her fingertips, she was extremely hot.

Looking down at the child, she had to fight tears so that she could do the necessary things to support her. Unfortunately, she felt helpless, and the dispatcher could offer her no more advice, since she was breathing and had a pulse.

Suddenly Morgan heard a male's voice calling out, "Hello? Anyone home? Snow White?"

She thought it was strange that she hadn't heard the sirens that signal an approaching ambulance, but was nonetheless relieved that help had arrived. "Back here," she called out as she went to the door to show the way. The man she saw, however, was not a medic. Taken aback, she realized that she could only now hear the faint wailing of sirens in the distance.

"Who are you?" he asked, a goofy grin on his face, as he walked down the hall, getting closer to where Morgan stood. Peeking around the corner, Morgan saw him walking down the hall, closer to Lucia's room. She felt extremely uneasy, and had the sudden urge to run away from him. As he leered at her and sauntered closer to her location, she chose to act on her instincts. Three seconds later, after she had locked the door, and as she was pushing the dresser in front of it, she heard him try the knob; when the lock held, he began banging very loudly against the two inches of wood that separated them. Her heart beat wildly as the insistent barrage became louder.

Suddenly, the racket stopped, and the man growled through the door, "You have something that belongs to me and I want it back!" When she made no move to allow him access, he accelerated his attempts at entry.

Between the pounding and screaming, Morgan heard that the sirens were slightly louder than before. She watched the door tremble with each new assault, and was terrified of what would happen once he forced his way in.

Looking around for something…anything to protect herself, she spotted an aluminum baseball bat in the corner of the room. Grabbing it, she looked toward Lucia and sent up a silent prayer of thanks that the girl was so out of it.

The pounding and screaming continued with renewed effort and force. Accompanying the reverberations of the door, she heard him screaming, "Who! The! Fuck! Are! You?!" with each screamed word accentuated by something hitting the door. Morgan knew it wouldn't hold much longer.

With the next volley, he threatened, "We have a place for cunts like you that get in the way, and they get hurt real good. If you give up my property now, I'll see to it that you get punished better than those other whores."

Morgan's hope grew as she realized that the sirens were now very close. Remembering that her previous 911 call had not included any mention of a homicidal madman, she dialed the familiar number again, setting her phone on the bed after turning on the speakerphone.

She worried that he would amp up his rampage once he heard the 911 operator coming from the phone inside the room. However, it was soon apparent that this would not be an issue as his latest assault drowned out any other noise altogether. Her assailant had evidently located a new weapon, as his continued ranting was punctuated by a chipping sound that brought to mind a varied range of sharp objects. Gashes soon appeared in the door; the first rents were small, but they quickly became larger with his repeated assaults.

Morgan's heart jumped into her throat when she could see his eye peeking in at her through the newly-created, rough-edged hole in the door. He looked crazed, and she was reminded of the look in her stalker's eyes…just before she put several bullets into his head. She looked down at the bat in her hands; she desperately wished that she had one of her guns near to hand. Her jaw set in determination, she choked up slightly on the bat, took a deep breath, and swung…hitting the hole right where his eye glared at her.

Flinching and surprised for a moment, he snarled, newly enraged. "You're gonna pay for that you fucking cunt, and then I'm gonna play with you real good. I might even save this knife and use it to play with you." His voice sounded raspy to Morgan, and she could smell his fetid breath through the hole in the door. She noted these things in split second intervals, as her brain took snapshots of her surroundings.

Where the fuck are the police? she wondered, feeling increasingly concerned as his knife made more progress in giving him access to her.

Finally, she heard a new voice from afar speaking loudly, and the madman's ranting and hacking stopped. She listened intently, working to interpret the situation on the other side of the door. Silence ensued, and then more loud voices, though it was difficult to make out specific words. She then heard a series of loud pops, followed by a muffled banging on her damaged barricade. She decided-hoped- that her assailant had been shot, as she somehow knew his silence would happen no other way. However, until she had verification, she wasn't opening the door.

After what seemed like ages, there was a knock. Suddenly, a different eye peeked through the destroyed door, and she heard a man announce, "Ma'am, this is the Oklahoma City Police Department. I need you to unlock the door."

Despite the calm nature of the voice, Morgan wasn't about to open that door until the identity of the voice's owner had been verified. "Step back from the door so that I can see your uniform," she requested, her voice surprisingly steady considering her shaky nerves.

To her surprise, he chuckled, but then did as requested. After looking through the hole and seeing the welcome and familiar police uniform, she frantically pulled the dresser out of the way and unlocked the door, throwing herself into his arms.

She wasted no time before pointing to Lucia and stammering that the girl needed help as she sobbed incoherently. Only then did she allow herself to be led into the hall by the officer who handled her hysterics with grace and understanding.

Upon exiting the room, she had to step over a bullet-riddled body that she was certain was her assailant's. As she moved past him, two thoughts entered her mind. First, he didn't look very big or ferocious, crumpled on the ground in a heap with his head resting on his chest and his mouth gaping open.

And second, he appeared quite relaxed, almost as if he was sleeping. The thoughts that rambled through her mind almost caused a hysterical laugh to escape, but the officer's prompting interrupted the deluge, and assisted her continued trek to exit the ransacked dwelling.

Passing Miss Dean's room, she looked in and noted that medics were already attending to her. Somewhere deep inside Morgan, an anger welled up; a stark rage that made her want to throttle the woman whose limp and lifeless body was being worked on. *How could that pitiful creature in there allow such a thing to happen?* she wondered, as she tamped down the fury that attempted to overwhelm her.

Finally outside, she breathed in the frigid February air and worked to calm herself. After watching both Lucia and Miss Dean being wheeled into an ambulance, a different officer than before approached her with something in his hand. Looking down, she numbly realized that he was asking if the phone he carried belonged to her. She nodded and palmed it, continuing to stare without seeing at the ground in front of her. After a while, she distantly thought that a body guard would probably not be such a bad thing.

Chapter Seven

Jasmine finally arrived in Indianapolis twelve hours later than anticipated, after stopping-involuntarily- in a hotel the previous night. It was also without Brunne or the children. The blizzard that had rolled through the Midwest was not a storm she wanted to risk having her children in, so she'd left them at the halfway point in St Louis. If she had been sensible, she knew she should have stayed as well. But there was no way she would be kept from Patrick any longer than necessary.

As she neared his location, her heart began beating faster and her palms started sweating. Checking her GPS, she saw that he was a block up and one over. Not that she could tell from the roads or the street signs; they were covered in layers of ice and snow. When she made it to her destination, she barely avoided skidding into a car, but managed to stop the vehicle just in time.

Looking up at the motel, Jasmine saw Patrick looking down at her. She decided that if she had to turn around right then, the overlarge smile that split his face in half would have made the trip worth it. She unbuckled her seat belt and ripped the door open, racing to him and jumping into his arms. The force of her body meeting his, coupled with the ice beneath his feet, caused him to slip; the two landed in a heap together.

Between their kisses, she could hear him laughing happily. Once the merriment subsided, his kisses deepened as his hand crept under her shirt. Soon she was breathing heavy from the pleasure of his touch. After caressing her for a moment longer, he pulled back, looking at her before announcing in his heavy Irish accent that he had to get her inside. After adjusting himself, he stood up and then helped her to her feet.

Opening the door to his room, Patrick pulled her in and began undressing her with an enthusiasm she had not experienced in a very long time. While he worked at her clothing, she managed to yank his shirt over his head. His pants, however, proved to be a bit more difficult, as his arousal made it next to impossible for her to unbutton them. He watched her for a time, amused; before long, however, the pressure must have been almost painful, as he decided to help her.

After freeing him from his trousers, Jasmine's mouth began to water as she looked at his large erection. He wasn't as big as John, thankfully; he fit her perfectly, and she couldn't wait to have him inside of her. However, he had other plans, and he pushed her back on the bed to put them into action.

"Oh my love, I want you inside me," she said, looking disappointed.

He ran his tongue lightly over his upper lip as his eyes travelled hungrily down her body, his gaze locking on his intended destination. However, the answering smile at her words told her clearly that he could deny her nothing, and he offered a compromise. "I canna stand not to have my face buried deep inside you, tasting ye here," he said, moving his finger over her sensitive nerves in a sensuous massage as a preview of things to come.

She closed her eyes to the onslaught of pleasure for a moment, but then agreed to his request by lying on her side and pulling his penis to her mouth. Pushing his hips towards her face with her palm, she then pulled his shaft between her lips. Before he could get his own mouth to the object of his desire, she began suckling him. As she took him into her mouth and then down her throat, he seemed to lose all thought regarding his former intentions, as he himself was lost in the sensations that she created.

Because of the way he shuddered as his breathing quickened, Jasmine sensed the effect she had on him. She took pleasure in it, loving the power she had over him, able to make his body come alive with desire. As the initial overwhelming intensity coalesced into a more even and divine pleasure, he moved closer and flicked his tongue, tentatively stroking her most sensitive spot. All breath rushed out of her lungs, and she had to pause the suction she was applying to absorb the fierce sensations that gripped her before continuing where she left off.

Eventually, the only sounds in the room were intermittent moans and continuous swishing of the bed sheets as the two writhed, making love with their mouths. As she continued her erotic tasting of Patrick, he also continued applying his own pressure, his tongue moving and flicking without pause. Soon, the pressure become so intense that she had to stop and cry out, "Patch! Inside me now!" through her gasping breaths. He was happy to oblige, wanting to spend his desire inside her feminine channel rather than her mouth.

He quickly turned around and then entered her, the sensations causing them both to moan as he slowly rode her. He remembered what she liked, and soon they were both hovering on the edge. With one last thrust, he pounded into her deeply and, with their faces buried in each other's necks, they both cried out. After being apart for so long, the two could do nothing but lie close to each other, enveloped within the other, while breathing in their lover's scent.

After spending an endless amount of time holding each other, they surfaced. Staring into each other's eyes, they were nearly breathless for having longed for a touch that did not come for far too long.

Finally, Patrick spoke, breaking the silence. "It has been too long, my beloved. How have I existed these years without you?" The time it took him to finish his statement was almost too long for Jasmine to hold back, and she violently pulled his face to hers and devoured his mouth. So deprived of the touch and love of the other, they couldn't get enough, and they nearly consumed one another, scarcely allowing time to breathe.

When their mouths were finally sated, they began grinding, pelvis against pelvis, until Patrick could no longer deny himself the pleasure of having her again. She returned his passion, pulling him in with her legs, desperately needing all of him. He entered her slowly, enjoying the feel of her, inch by inch. Her moans told him that he was right where she wanted him. When he moved rhythmically inside her, it was luxuriously slow, every stroke accentuated by him tasting her mouth.

It had often been this way during their lovemaking. He didn't pound into her the way that John often did; he was more eager to draw it out, each sensuous moment cherished, rather than building up a raging inferno that was so overwhelming that she quickly lost herself. Patrick took his time, building a pace that was more suited to her, fitting her in exactly the way only her perfect partner could.

Jasmine couldn't help but express the intense emotions she felt. "Oh my love, I've missed your touch so much." He brought his mouth to her breast, his tongue circling caresses over her nipples.

Lifting his head, he looked her in the eye and said, "I can't believe you are here with me at last. I have for so long dreamt of being with you like this." After expressing this sentiment, neither could speak. They were overcome with a palpable need for each other. Their desire not yet spent, they thrust into each other over and over, finishing together in a seemingly eternal moment of ecstasy. Eventually, they collapsed on the bed together, trying to pull oxygen into their lungs.

Finally, they lay still together and fell asleep, exhausted and exhilarated from the workout they'd just had.

****

When the police had finally finished interviewing Morgan, it was late in the evening, and John was waiting for her in front of the police station. He allowed time for her to settle herself into the passenger seat before reaching over and hugging her. Adjusting the driver's seat, he then picked her up and pulled her onto his lap so that she was squeezed snuggly between the steering wheel and his torso.

"My love, I was so worried about you!" he exclaimed, kissing and embracing her tightly. The violent trembling began in her body and shook the two as they sat embracing each other. Considering what she had just been through, it was obviously unrelated to the cold front that had moved in earlier that day.

They sat silently for several intense moments while she clung to him. Finally, she told him, "I've got to get to the hospital, John."

He nodded his understanding and helped her return to the passenger seat. "I only ask that you stay with me afterwards, so that I can care for you and see to your safety." It was her turn to nod. Putting the car in gear, he drove them to Children's Hospital.

When Morgan checked her phone, she saw that she had several missed calls and texts from Stacia. Her daughter was obviously anxious for news of her friend. Morgan couldn't call her yet, however; at least not until she knew the status of Lucia's condition. She decided that delaying a call to her daughter was a better option than sharing incomplete information.

When they were close to their destination, her phone began buzzing. *Probably Stacia again,* she thought resignedly. When she checked the caller ID, however, she recognized Maggie's number. She barely had time to grunt before Maggie bombarded her with, "I have a really bad feeling, Morgan. What's happening?" Though surprised, Morgan wasn't shocked. Her best friend often seemed to have uncanny premonitions when things were dire; her impossible insight had proven itself often enough in the past.

"It's Lucia," Morgan told her, explaining the recent developments. By the time she had finished recounting the story, she and John were already at Lucia's bedside in the pediatric ICU. Mag said that she was on her way.

Seeing the child, barely fifteen years old, with tubes going in and out, as well as a machine breathing for her…it was difficult to say the least. It was all Morgan could do to resist picking her up and holding her. Memories of her as a little girl in kindergarten; watching the happy child grow up throughout elementary school…the thoughts flooded in, and she had to constantly swallow the tears that threatened to choke her. John, seeing her distress, rubbed her shoulders until Lucia's nurse came to speak with them.

As the nurse spoke with her and painted a clinical picture of Lucia's condition, Morgan was distracted by seeing Dr. Schambaugh walk through the door, obviously there to check on the child during his rounds. She felt an immediate sense of irritation. Not only did his presence seem to bode poorly for Lucia's prognosis, but she didn't want him around Maggie; he seemed to have an unusual attachment to her friend. Mag needed no other complications in her life at the moment.

"Hello, I'm Dr. Schambaugh, the neurology Fellow…" He broke off the introduction abruptly, recognizing Morgan from their previous meetings. "You have had a tragic week," he observed, speaking to Morgan while shaking John's hand.

"What's going on with her?" she asked, ignoring the niceties and motioning to Lucia with her chin.

The doctor took a deep breath before answering. "Do you have any idea where she could've gotten ecstasy from?" Dr. Schambaugh appeared hesitant to share the troublesome news that Lucia had taken the drug, obviously wanting to be delicate and sympathetic. Morgan's opinion of him went up marginally.

"I have no idea where she could've gotten that or why she would be doing it by herself." Morgan rubbed her eyes as she answered, exasperated by both the current situation and the recent stresses she had gone through. When she pulled her hand away, she saw that Mag had arrived, and she reached out to hug her best friend.

"Ecstasy?" Mag asked, overhearing the conversation as she walked in. Upon hearing the newcomer enter, the doctor turned toward her and seemed to forget everyone else in the room for the moment as the two stared at one another.

The moment quickly became awkward, and John cleared his throat; looking in his direction, both Maggie and Dr. Schambaugh seemed to remember that they weren't alone. "What was I saying?" the doctor continued, covering his embarrassment. "Oh yes, ecstasy. She also had valium in her system. Right now, we have placed her in a medically-induced coma to preserve brain function as we work to reduce her fever. She had a toxic level of MDMA in her system, and it caused her to overheat. The valium actually probably helped by preventing a seizure."

He paused a moment to allow the news to register, and then continued. "We won't know the extent of the damage until she wakes, which we can't allow until we stabilize her. I suspect tomorrow we will be able to turn the Propofol off and bring her out of the coma. Then we will see where she stands regarding brain function."

Morgan hugged herself while shaking her head, upset that the child was in such a horrible situation, and wondering if there was something she could have done to prevent it. John saw her distress and stepped up behind her, wrapping his arms around her and pulling her against him.

The room was silent as the gravity of Lucia's situation sunk in.

The pause in the conversation allowed Maggie to see all of the other occupants in the room. She noticed the way the stranger embraced her best friend- so caringly and protectively- and decided that he must be John. She watched the lovers longingly, wishing she had someone who loved her that way.

As Maggie watched her friend, Dr. Schambaugh studied her before requesting, "Can we talk outside?"

Morgan stared after her friend as she followed the doctor out, curiosity tinged with speculation visible on her face.

After exiting the ICU bay, the doctor took a sharp left and led Maggie through an isolated hallway to a small room labeled **Resident Call Room**. He moved to the keypad next to the door, punched in a code, and then held the door open for her. Maggie looked at him questioningly, while standing her ground on the threshold of the room.

"I wanted to discuss the girl's case away from your friend, as well as your mother's passing in private, away from others in the ICU." She frowned slightly. "HIPAA," he offered in way of explanation, which prompted her to enter. Her expression cleared, and she entered the room, smiling slightly in embarrassment at her unwanted suspicion.

Once inside, he motioned for her to sit in the lone chair just inside the cramped room. After propping the door open, he sat on the edge of the twin bed across from the chair so that he could face Maggie as they talked. "How are you holding up since your mother's passing?"

Startled by the personal nature of the question, she blinked at him before answering, "I'm doing much better than I would've thought. Thank you for letting me know that I gave her good care, Dr. Schambaugh. It was killing me to think I caused her death."

"Please, call me Dave." He patted her knee and awaited her affirming nod before continuing. "Yes, the work you did with her should be documented and taught in medical text books, or discussed in medical journals, to say the least. Would you be opposed to working a project with me so that I can do a write up about it?"

She noticed that his hand remained on her knee. However, after witnessing the intimacy between

Morgan and John, she enjoyed the contact immensely, and allowed his hand to remain. He made heavy eye contact with her as he spoke. Maggie found herself blushing and had difficulty looking away from him. A part of her wished he would kiss her right there in the secluded call room.

"I would love that!" Maggie exclaimed, feeling slightly flushed as she stared at him. When he leaned toward her, her heart jumped and she unconsciously licked her lower lip. He broke eye contact for the first time as his gaze shifted to her mouth, staring at her slightly glistening lips.

He stopped moving abruptly. After a few moments of awkward silence, he looked at her speculatively and mused, in a whisper, "I really want to kiss you right now."

She released her breath in a rush as their mouths met hungrily, devouring each other. As she leaned into him, losing herself in the kiss, he pulled her forward onto his lap. The kiss deepened as he wrapped his arms around her, both of them breathless. Their bodies were so close…total access with only their clothing as barriers. Their hands soon found their way, each touching and exploring the other. The tension in the room had built to a nearly palpable force, when he abruptly stood, picking her up in one motion as he reached for the door, slamming it closed.

She wrapped her legs around his waist, locking them there while he laid her gently on the bed. Her legs found their way around his waist and locked there until he laid her on the bed. He hovered over her, looking down at her face. She watched him watching her…and knew that she couldn't wait to see and feel more of him.

"Take your shirt off," he whispered, beating her to it. "I want to look at you when I take you." She complied as he continued to study her. He then lightly placed pressure on her shoulders until she laid back on the narrow twin bed. Only then did he untie his scrub pants.

She watched as he began to stroke himself, raising her eyes to look up at his unwavering gaze. Huskily, he instructed her, "Fondle yourself. I want you wet for me." As he placed his hands at her waist, unbuttoning her pants, she swirled her fingertips over her nipples tantalizingly. Leaning to the side, he reached under the mattress and retrieved a condom. Quickly rolling the rubber sheath onto himself, he announced, "I'm going to enjoy the shit out of this." He then entered her, taking her nipple into his mouth in the process.

While he thrust into her, her hands roamed over his pecs, then moved to his shoulders, until finally settling on his back. She was so starved for intimate contact that it didn't take her long to start moaning, assisting enthusiastically with each thrust. She felt her orgasm building. Suddenly, however, he stopped pumping into her, placing his hands on each of her hips and holding her still. "Stop moving for a sec," he whispered. "I just want to feel you." She smiled up at him sweetly without moving, savoring his invasion of her.

Finally, he started pumping into her again, and she moaned into his mouth as he leaned down and kissed her. His movements built an exquisite pressure, and the intensity soared even higher for her. She enjoyed the sensation as he stoked the fire within her... she felt like she was reaching for something exquisite that was just out of her grasp. Abruptly, with a last jerky thrust, he shuddered on top of her, going deeper than any of his previous movements had taken him.

When he finished, he leaned down, kissed her forehead, and then withdrew from her. She continued to lie there for a moment, noting the agonizing sensations of her body with a feeling of unfulfilled frustration. She tried to process what had just occurred, feeling slightly confused. Suddenly, she noticed him standing over her. "We should probably go back now," he said, reaching down to help her up. She took his hand as he assisted her, and they moved toward their destination together, in awkward silence, while she straightened her shirt.

When they returned to the ICU bay, Morgan looked at her questioningly until Dr. Schambaugh announced, "Thank you for your time, Miss Sumner. If there's anything else I can do to help with your mother's arrangements, I trust that you'll let me know."

Maggie saw Morgan's eyes narrow as she cleared her throat. Her friend then insisted, "Yes, her mom, great! Is there something you can tell me about the current patient, Lucia?"

Dr Schambaugh, unperturbed, looked at the child and explained, "As I was saying earlier, the next forty-eight hours will be telling. Unfortunately, until we are able to bring her out of her coma, we will not know how she will do. On one hand, she can make a full recovery. But at the other end of the spectrum, she may remain in a persistent vegetative state once she surfaces. I will certainly keep you updated on her status, Miss…" he prompted Morgan to give her name.

When her friend was not forthcoming, Maggie stepped in to fill the silence. "Freeman. It's Miss Freeman…Morgan, my best friend." Maggie introduced her friend, not wanting the man she had just had intimate relations with to be under fire. "And Morgan, this is Dr. Schambaugh…David."

The doctor nodded at Morgan, acknowledging the introduction, but then looked past her to John. "And you are?" he prompted.

John stepped out from behind Morgan and shook the doctor's hand, looking him up and down in silent appraisal. "I am John Kennedy. Morgan's boyfriend," he announced, as he stepped between his woman and the man she obviously distrusted. Morgan seemed surprised by his proclamation of their relationships status, but she schooled her features as John's stance was protective of her. She then glanced toward Maggie, perhaps trying to gauge her reaction.

Maggie was too busy watching the interplay between the doctor and John, tension in the room heightening, to fully process the words that were spoken. "Did you say John Kennedy?" the doctor asked. Before John could answer, he prompted, "*The* John Kennedy of Ireland?" John looked him up and down again as if trying to figure out how the complete stranger before him knew of him.

Before either man could comment, Maggie spoke up and directed a question at the doctor. "Before we discuss who Morgan's man is, could you give us some idea on Lucia?" She had said the first bit more forcefully than she intended, and softened the last part to compensate.

When the group turned to look at Maggie, she elaborated, "What I mean is, what is the criteria for bringing her out of her coma? Will it be when her vital signs continue to show stability, or is there a set amount of time until the decision is made no matter what? If my friend has an idea about that, she will probably feel much better, and you will be one hundred times less likely to receive a thousand phone calls in the middle of the night. And my friend would be one of those patient's family members to persistently call you. Believe me!"

Her comment diffused the uncomfortable tension, and the doctor answered, "Ah yes. That makes sense. I believe the plan is to start weaning her at noon tomorrow. That'll be more than eighteen known hours that she has been out. Research and evidence proves it to be the best timeframe for bringing the individual poisoned from this substance out of the medically necessary coma. One of the drawbacks of being unable to speak with the patient, however, is that we don't know for sure how much MDMA she ingested."

Finally seeming satisfied with the information offered, Morgan thanked him. She then sat on the chair next to the child she'd known for more than a decade. John and Dr. Schambaugh stepped outside to talk, leaving the two best friends alone with the little girl.

Once the men were away, Morgan looked to her friend and asked, "Where did ya'll go? You were gone a really long time."

Maggie looked down at her and rubbed her shoulder. "It's the whole privacy thing with medical care," she lied. "He was asking me about my mom's health history. He's doing a study on the possible causes of MS. He thinks there could be a genetic component involved in how well she survived the disease, so…" She trailed off, hoping her best friend would buy it.

As Morgan turned her head to look at her, Maggie massaged harder, prompting her to turn back toward the comatose child. Maggie had to swallow her guilt and push down her doubts about what had transpired. *It was just meaningless sex,* she told herself. Belying the thought, she had been single for a very long time…the human contact felt nice.

Her mind shifted to the idea of being with David: an accomplished doctor with whom she would have something in common. They would probably never run out of things to talk about. She knew she was being a silly girl, fantasizing about things that she had no business dreaming about, but the idea gave her a high that made her current situation tolerable.

Her thoughts ended abruptly when John and David returned. John went to Morgan and picked her up, sitting down with her on his lap. Maggie watched him whisper into her friend's ear as she snuggled into his chest. Maggie couldn't fail to notice that he held her close to himself in a protective embrace.

"I'll leave you folks alone for now," Dr Schambaugh said.

As he exited the ICU room, Maggie followed him to the nurse's station, politely requesting, "Will you please call us if anything changes?"

He set down the chart he was perusing and looked down at her pensively. After taking a deep breath, he answered with a small grin, "It would be my pleasure, Maggie Sumner." As he lightly yanked a few strands of her hair. "What is your number? I look forward to speaking with you again." She took the pen that was proffered and, turning his left hand over, wrote her number on his palm while giving what she hoped was a sultry smile.

In Lucia's ICU bay, John whispered in Morgan's ear, "My love, you are swaying and having difficulty holding your head up, you are so exhausted. Let me take you away from here so that I can assure that you rest, and care for you properly."

She snuggled into his neck as she replied, "I don't want to leave her. I feel like I'm all she has." She closed her eyes and inhaled his clean masculine scent.

While rubbing her neck with one hand he used the other to push her hair out of her face as he kissed her. "You heard what the doctor said, Morgan. She will remain in her deep sleep until tomorrow. It will do her no good for you to wear yourself out. Please, doll, I have rented a room close to here for us. We can be here quickly if anything changes."

Morgan rubbed her eyes as she considered his words. With her eyes closed she could feel her overwhelming exhaustion, and she knew that her lover spoke the truth. As he continued to massage her neck and shoulders, the tension began to drain from her, and her weariness hit her like a ton of bricks.

Fuck! she thought, wondering when her life had become so complicated and so…tragic. She kept thinking that life wasn't supposed to be this way. She couldn't keep her mind off of the unbelievable death toll that had begun to surround her of late. Was it a sign, or an omen? She tried not to think that way as she soaked up the sensations from her lover's crafty hands.

Though John had waited patiently while she was lost in her reverie, he finally prompted, "Please, *ma shearc*." He whispered the words in her ear, following them with a soft nip of his teeth. She placed her palm flat against his chest and looked up at him. After staring at each other for an eternity, they leaned in and kissed. Then, hugging him, she conceded,

"You are right of course. Thank you for looking out for me, John," before standing up next to him and preparing to leave.

Maggie chose that moment to return. Sensing that Morgan was preparing to leave, she stated, "I'm glad you're going. You look like you're about to fall over." The two women hugged, leaning into each other, until Mag reassured her, "He will call me if anything changes, and you will be the first person I call, Morgan. Go…get some sleep. I promise I will call you."

John shook Maggie's hand while holding onto Morgan supportively. "It was nice to meet you... Maggie?" he asked, a dark eyebrow quirked.

Morgan gasped. "I'm so sorry," she exclaimed. "With everything, I forgot to introduce the two of you."

Before she could continue, John waved away her remorse and stated, "My little love, you have been through in the past week enough to make Gandhi go insane. Besides, no introductions are necessary. It is quite obvious that this is your best friend, Maggie." He said this with a slight bow, and then continued, "And I am very thankful that she cares quite a bit about you and loves you very much. I can see why, despite the constant peril that surrounds you, you have managed to stay alive for so long."

Mag blushed under his attention, enjoying John's chivalrous nature; she obviously approved of Morgan's choice. "It's lovely to meet you, John. I've heard a lot about you, and I'm glad you're taking my friend away for her own good…otherwise she would stay with the child until she comes out of it. She's too caring for her own damn good sometimes." She said this last bit fiercely, but Morgan also heard a mixture of reproach, pride, and love in her friend's voice.

To Morgan's disgruntlement, John agreed. The two friends hugged one last time. Exhausted, the three moved toward the door. The two friends hugged one last time before parting.

As Maggie walked from Lucia's room into the hallway, she came to an abrupt halt as she noticed Dr. Schambaugh waiting for her. He motioned, asking her to follow him one last time further down the hall.

"When can I see you again?" he asked, holding her arm so that she remained close to him. For a moment, Mag felt as though he had put her on the spot. However, as he began caressing her arm in slow circles, she soon relaxed and allowed him to hold her in place. Smiling at his request, she answered, "Soon I hope." She kissed his cheek gently. "Call me when you're away from work," she followed up as she made her way to the elevator.

Chapter Eight

Surfacing in pitch black- in an unfamiliar bed and in a tangle of arms and legs- Jasmine thought for a fraction of a second that John had forgiven her and that they'd gone away somewhere together. The scent that found her nose, however, was an altogether different smell than John's. Snapping back to the present, she moved her body against Patrick's. He awoke instantly, reacting to her, pulling her into his developing erection.

"I want you to bite me, lover," she informed him breathily. He seemed surprised at her request; when he hesitated, she pulled his head to her breast and directed him in a whisper, "Nibble me lightly here, and then lick it." He did as instructed, causing her to moan and rub against him like a cat.

Sensing his mounting tension, she looked down and saw that he was studying her face with a look of concern. "Jasmine, when did ye start wanting *this*?" He emphasized the last word with a sound of disappointment. His question gave her pause, and for the first time in his presence, she felt ashamed.

"I…I…Patrick, I'm sorry," she stammered. "It's something John started doing since the last time you and I were together."

The hurt was clearly visible on his face, and he abruptly sat up in the middle of the bed. "Jasmine, why would ye bring him into our lovemaking?" he asked, moving away from her on the bed.

"Please don't move away from me, Patrick," she pleaded as she reached for him at the edge of the bed. Standing up, he began pacing, in an obvious attempt to avoid her. Jasmine buried her face in her hands as silent tears fell into her palms.

Patrick turned to her reluctantly, the pain clear in his plaintive face. "I don't understand. Why do ye want me, if ye want me to be like me brother when I make love to ya?" She kept her face covered and couldn't look at him when he spoke. Instead, in answer, she began rocking back and forth, an involuntary sob escaping. He stopped pacing and looked over at her, appearing only now to truly see her in her misery and shame.

Feeling his weight on the mattress next to her, she brought her head up to stare into his eyes. She felt as though he was looking right into her soul, and they sat studying each other for what felt like hours. Finally, he broke the spell and brought his hand to her face, wiping her tears in a loving caress. She placed her palm over his hand and held it to her cheek. With heartfelt regret, she whispered, "I'm sorry my darling. It seems I am destined to hurt those I love the most."

In response to her apology, he slowly pulled her toward himself and kissed her gently on the forehead. She closed her eyes, breathing him in and cherishing his touch. As his lips moved down her face, she opened her eyes and watched him, thinking, *Please let this be okay. Please let him make love to me again.*

When his lips met hers, it began as a chaste kiss that quickly deepened, so that his tongue entered her mouth, causing her breath to escape in a rush. She returned his affection by moving into him as she twisted her tongue around his.

As Patrick tasted his Jasmine, his need to feel more of her was evident, as if he wanted to crawl into her skin and never leave. As he continued to deepen the kiss, he wrapped his arms around her waist, pulling her onto his lap. Her thigh brushed his hardening shaft, causing them both to moan. She had always had this effect on him; while they were together, he perpetually had an erection. He had often been unaware of this fact, only to be brought to a complete understanding of the havoc she wreaked on his body by no more than a slight, soft rub.

"I love you so much, Jasmine," he professed. "Please forgive me for pulling away. I just…my brother has had you for so long. Now that I finally have you, the thought of all of the time I missed while you were with him…" Looking into his eyes, she could see the same loneliness that she felt, caused by a long absence from each other. Chasing the painful memories away, he kissed her as she snuggled more closely against him.

Laying her back, he climbed on top of her, parting her thighs with his body. She was already wet for him, and he seemed to be on a mission to taste her. After kissing her mouth, he trailed kisses down her neck, and then continued his downward path. He leisurely stopped at her nipples, licking first one, and then the other. She was so responsive to him, swollen with need as always, and her hips pressed against his chest as she savored the feel of his mouth on her breast. After paying the hardened buds of her nipples the proper attention, he continued his journey to the warm haven between her legs. The first swipe of his tongue caused her to moan pleadingly, pushing herself more firmly against his mouth.

"Oh Patrick, my love!" she exclaimed. As he tasted the nectar she exuded, she pumped her hips, riding his face as the pleasure built for both of them. Fisting her hands in his rich chestnut hair, she anchored herself when the sensations became too much. Quickly her complete attention was riveted to the sole task of coping with the overwhelming pleasure. Involuntarily, she began turning her head from side to side as her hips bucked, shoving her pelvis more firmly into his mouth.

"Patch, I need you inside me!" She barely managed to get the words out, entranced in pleasure as she was. He needed no further prompting, and he quickly perched on his knees, entering her with an exquisite slowness, filling her inch by inch. As he pulled her hips toward himself, he buried himself inside of her. She pushed against the headboard as they came together, slowly, but with delicious pressure, and they both called out, moaning and breathless.

Their erotic dance continued, building with intensity and pleasure over and over with each thrust of their hips. Jasmine couldn't help but think of how different her lover was from her husband. Patrick liked to take it slow, savoring the feel of her as he moved in and out, as if committing every centimeter of her body he had contact with to memory. He often accentuated each inward movement with a kiss; either on her breasts, or her neck, or her mouth. John was wilder in his pursuit of sexual satisfaction.

When they were both close, Patrick brought his mouth to hers and kissed her deeply. As she climaxed, she bit his lip, sucking it into her mouth. She then thrust her tongue into his mouth as his seed jetted into her.

Breathless, he collapsed on top of her.

Lying next to each other, finally catching their breaths, Patrick broke the silence by whispering into her ear, "There is nothing better than being inside ye, me sweet." She looked over at him and smiled blissfully, happy to have her lover in her arms after such a long separation. After a soft kiss full of meaning and devotion, she snuggled into him and they drifted off to sleep in each other's arms.

****

When Morgan and John arrived at The Ambassador, where John had rented a hotel room for them, she was surprised to discover that it was only ten o'clock in the evening. As he ran the shower for her, she felt the tiredness sink into her bones; she wanted nothing more than to sleep for the next month and to put the tragedies of the last week behind her. While she sat in the room's only chair, the overwhelming exhaustion overtook her and she fell into the oblivion of sleep.

She drifted to the precipice of wakefulness as John laid her softly onto the bed, but became more alert as she felt his caress on her cheek. She couldn't resist the temptation of holding him close to her as he kissed her chin and they held each other close. As his arms held her, she ached with need for his embrace and his touch.

While John gripped her tight, she buried her face into his chest. Although she fought it, she couldn't hold back the tears or the sobs that emerged, suddenly racking her body, the stresses of recent days unleashing a new torrent. The repressed anguish and terror exploded out of her as he brushed the hair away from her face, kissing at her tears. She fell apart in his arms, rocked by her uncontrollable emotions, her body convulsing. He was steady as a rock, continuing to hold her, the embodiment of stability that she so desperately needed in her swirling chaos.

Morgan burrowed into his chest, finding sanctuary in the security she found there. Soon, however, as the storm passed, she realized she needed more. She moved against him, wanting to convey her desperate desire. Perceptive as ever, he immediately registered the change in her breathing and her plaintive caress, understanding her urgency. She loved that he didn't disappoint her in her time of need.

As her mouth met his chest, she felt his nipple brush against her lips, and she extended her tongue, swirling the flattened nub until it hardened. His breath hissed out at the contact, and he looked down at her, meeting her fevered stare. Bringing his mouth to hers, he kissed her- chastely at first, testing, awaiting her silent affirmation. Her breathing quickened as she bared her desire for him; her need for what he offered, reflecting his obvious need to be buried deeply within her. Her body moved against his, and she moaned into his mouth as she felt his engorged penis push tentatively against her through the fabric of his pants.

"Please, John, I need you," she moaned, parting her legs, seeking to pull him into her. He was happy to oblige. Pushing his pants down and away from his waist, he released himself. His manhood sprung away from his hips abruptly, stopping just at her entrance as if programmed to go there. He kissed her again, this time more deeply, as he repositioned himself on his elbows, poised and readying himself to enter her.

Before doing so, he paused, appearing to study Morgan's face, perhaps needing to see the yearning she felt for him...to see and not just hear how fully she desired him. Evidently seeing what he required, he surged forward, eliciting a throaty moan from her ravenous mouth. He then made love to her slowly, rhythmically moving in and out.

As he continued thrusting himself, the intensity built for both of them; they desperately needed to find release. Like the raging storm of her emotions, the pleasure flew out of control as they frantically moved into each other.

Together, they stood on the edge of the precipice for one agonizing moment...and then they exploded together, each echoing the other's cries. Spent, Morgan lay back, breathless, with John on top of her, the two absorbing their combined essence. Unable to move, they could do nothing more than breathe for the moment; the world did not exist as they enjoyed the sensation of each other's bodies. After the longest time, they both drifted into oblivion as sleep overtook them.

****

As the early morning light peeked in through the curtains, Jasmine slowly stretched before pulling herself closer to Patrick. Opening his eyes, he kissed her lips, touching her face as her gaze slowly focused on him. "My darling dear," his voice caressed her soul as his fingers caressed her face. "I am famished, so I know it must be so for you. It is time that I feed ye, me love." She soaked up his attention, rising and kissing his lips once more.

"What do you have in mind my beloved?" she asked, anticipating something delicious; he had a way with food in conjunction with making love. He evidently saw her excitement as he looked down at her face. Joyfully, he bent down and suckled her bottom lip, savoring the taste of her. She returned his affection, rubbing herself against his thigh until they were breathless, the fire building for them both.

It didn't take much kissing and rubbing before Patrick's need to enter her became undeniable. He thrust into her, and Jasmine met his pulsating hips by pushing her body against his. "My goddess, your body is so exquisite," he said between ragged breaths. "I can't get enough of being inside you."

Passionately, he rocked back and forth inside of her, accompanied by the building crescendo of her moans. He continued to stoke the fire until neither could take the intensifying pleasure for one more moment. With a final thrust, he settled into her, all the while tasting her mouth and capturing the moans that tried to escape from her.

When Jasmine managed to catch her breath, she looked down at his face, buried against her breast, and exclaimed to the top of his head, "My love, I am famished! What are we getting to eat?" She wondered what culinary delights he might have in mind.

After withdrawing and rising, Patrick looked down at her, his eyes meeting hers, and he seemed eager to please. "It is a surprise, my precious one... you will have to wait and see. But I promise, you will enjoy it, and find it exceptionally titillating." His last words were slightly muffled as he had leaned down and circled his tongue over her bared nipple, caressing. Her breath caught in her throat.

"I am sure I would find anything that you imagine to be well above satisfaction," she uttered as she pulled his head toward her face, stroking his ear with the tip of her tongue. By reflex, he moved to hover over her, his leg over her body possessively as he enjoyed her gentle caresses. With pleasure, Jasmine knew that he wanted to take her all over again.

Jasmine mused about her wonderfully newfound situation; Patrick knew her…knew of the damage inside of her. But still, he seemed to consider her a beautiful creature, perfect of form. She knew that he was poised, ready to enjoy the gift she offered. She warmed with the silent knowledge that he would always cherish any offer she made, staying with her until they both wasted away should she wish it. Smiling lasciviously, she bit his lip and pushed at his chest, sending him on his way. He would do as she prompted, providing sustenance for the two of them with one of his magnificent creations.

As calculated, he looked down at her with a knowing visage, before standing up and setting to work dressing himself. "I won't be gone for long, m'love," he told her in his beautiful and thick Irish accent, his face descending and brushing lightly over her lips.

As he walked outside, the door closing behind him, she lay under the sheets they had just so thoroughly used and enjoyed, reveling in the feel of her body…along with the twangs of pain she could feel in the delicate parts of her tissue, reminders of all of the pleasurable things they had done. She knew he would be gone for a while, and she wanted to continue experiencing the feelings of pleasure he had inspired.

When she touched herself, it was easy to pretend it was her Patrick, so fully satisfying her and giving her the pleasure that her body wanted… that her sensual and spiritual essence desired. As she touched and sensed her body, exploring the sensitive nerve endings and the delicious soreness, she pictured Patrick's face. She couldn't hold back the moan that escaped when she remembered the way he had touched her, as though worshipping her body.

As Jasmine continued to feel herself up, hands exploring her own nakedness and tweaking her nipples, a stray thought entered her mind- a scene from her recent session with John and their shared lover. Her hands stopped suddenly. *Why did I do that?* she thought, alarmed. *I must tell Patrick.* Her mind reeled with a horrible sense of dread, a knot forming in her stomach, and she couldn't stop the tears from falling. She couldn't make the sick feeling go away. She hated that she had to share the sickening news with her beloved. The temptation to keep silent was strong…but she knew that she couldn't keep it from him.

Chapter Nine

Awakening next to the man she loved, Morgan let out a deep sigh and snuggled closer to him. Squinting at the clock on the bedside table, she saw that it was nearly ten a.m. For a moment she thought to get up in a rush and hurry to the hospital; but when she looked over at John's peacefully sleeping face, she couldn't bring herself to do it. She took her time studying his profile, appreciating the raw masculine beauty she saw there. Needing to touch him, she stroked his chest with her fingertips.

Her eyes ascending his face, she saw that he was watching her intently. "I didn't mean to wake you, my love," she confessed, as her fingertips swirled caresses over his five o'clock shadow, lazily making their way to his cheek.

John closed his eyes as he savored her touch, breathing her in. After inhaling her scent deeply, he brought his mouth to hers and kissed her, a dying men quenching his thirst. Once satisfied, he broke the delicious contact, catching her eye and announcing, "I want to help you into the shower, and then we should go see your young friend at the hospital."

She soaked up his attention, and then answered, "I would love a hot shower right now before I check on the beloved child that is my daughter's lifetime friend." Taking the cue, he kissed her chin before pulling away from her, moving toward the bathroom.

After a moment, he emerged from the bathroom and brought her fully awake with the power of his kisses. "I am ready to wash you, my love," he announced, gathering her into his arms and moving toward the readied and heated shower. Morgan snuggled against his chest as his cautious steps carried her to the awaiting mist emanating from the faucet.

When they arrived, she thought he would surely set her down; to her surprise, however, he stepped over the barrier of the bathtub, still sheltering her in his arms. As he set her down and she felt the ceramic of the tub and the cascade of water, he continued to hold her close. "You have had an eventful week, *ma shearc*. Let me wash you," he murmured, advancing slowly.

She nodded against his chest as he pivoted, grabbing the shampoo and squirting it into his palm. Deliciously, she felt him spread the cool gel onto her scalp. As he massaged and rubbed, she continued to melt into him while pulling him closer. As he continued his work, she rested her cheek against his chest and began purring.

"I love taking care of you, my darling," he whispered into her hair as his hands moved in soft circles on top of her head. He then moved to the sides, rubbing her temples briefly before running his hands down to her neck. She soaked it all in as she sank against him, his cleansing ritual continuing.

When her hair had been thoroughly washed, John leaned down and retrieved the body wash, so conveniently placed by his hand earlier, she had no doubt. Squirting a glob into his hand and lathering it up, he started with her shoulders, kneading and working out the knots of tension. She closed her eyes, absorbing the feelings and scents that swirled around her.

"Thank you, darling," she breathed into the hollow of his shoulder. She exhaled with sheer bliss. She needed him to know the true depth of her gratitude. "…For taking such amazing care of me… and for letting me lose it for a minute."

He pulled away from her momentarily, staring down at her face with a look of pure empathy, before kissing her thoroughly. "My love, it gives me great pleasure to care for you." He accentuated the last word with a light tug on her hair, to which she responded by grinding her hip into his shaft, noting that he was beginning to harden.

His impish grin sent a shiver down Morgan's spine. She watched his mouth as it advanced closer, nervously biting her lower lip. He suddenly pulled her face to his, suckling her with his mouth, causing her to release the lip in a gasp of complete joy. Closing their eyes and inhaling deeply, they breathed one another in. When his hands finally moved over her back, she leaned against his chest while he completed his task of washing her.

Morgan's eyes were closed when he turned off the water, and she didn't see when he reached for a towel; but she soon felt the softness of the cotton as he brought it to her sensitive skin, drying her with gentle swipes. When she was dry from head to toe, he whispered in her ear, "We should go see your young friend now." She looked up at him and nodded.

****

At the hospital, Maggie and Morgan arrived simultaneously, with John standing protectively close by. It was also at the same time Dr. Schambaugh had begun working to bring Lucia out of her coma. "We decided to start early," he explained to their surprised expressions. "It often takes time for the sedation drugs to wear off."

Maggie walked up to the bed and, looking down at the vial in the doctor's hand, demanded,

"What is that, and why weren't we notified that this was happening ahead of time?"

Dr. Schambaugh sat the medicine on the table before turning to her. He then said, "She has been on Propofol. We stopped the medicine fifteen minutes ago and will watch her closely and extubate as soon as she begins fighting the breathing tube." He enunciated each word, answering as if challenging her to disagree with him.

When Maggie showed her intent to argue about the premature care, he sighed loudly and asked her, "Can I speak with you outside?" It was more a statement than a question, and he left the room, obviously expecting Maggie to obey. As she turned to follow him, her face on fire, she pointedly avoided the eyes of her best friend, as well as everyone else in the room.

She located him, down the hall, standing in a small cubby hole that contained a cart and a computer. He gestured for her to stand in the corner before demanding, "Miss Sumner, can I ask why you saw fit to question my medical judgment in front of the girl's friends and family?"

As she looked up at him, her heart jumped into her throat and she couldn't catch her breath. Obviously unsatisfied with her response, the doctor grabbed her upper arm. Wincing, she fully expected to be struck. However, he then brought his face close to hers. She continued to stare at him until he broke eye contact, pulling her in for a kiss. She tasted his passion, returning it without restraint as her hands groped his hip and his back. She pulled him tightly against herself.

Without warning, they heard footsteps approaching. Abruptly, he pulled away and announced over-loudly, "So you see Miss Sumner, Lucia will likely start to awaken shortly, and then we will have an idea about…" He broke off as soon as the passing medical aid was out of earshot. In a more normal tone, he confessed, "Sorry about that. I just can't seem to control myself around you."

She was breathless for a moment and it took her several heartbeats to collect her thoughts. Before she managed to speak, however, he made a request. "Maggie, I wanted to ask you a question. That is…I have a medical gala coming up this weekend and I wanted to take someone special with me…someone I can carry a conversation with that won't bore me to tears." As he spoke to her, he tucked stray hairs behind her ear before letting his hand rest on her shoulder.

The idea of being alone with him on a date- and in a public setting- was exciting, and she immediately nodded. She was charmed, appreciating the way he looked at her, as well as admiring his accomplishments and status as an established specialty physician.

Her concentration was broken when he prompted, "Well?"

When she still couldn't find her voice, he cleared his throat and pinched her side, making her jump slightly. She blinked and focused on him, stuttering, "Yeah, go with you…to dinner. I can do that." His answering smile left her breathless, and for a moment her anxiety spiked.

Pulling her gently by the arm back toward the ICU room, he reiterated, "Okay, great. So, Friday night I'll pick you up. It's a date." When they drew close to Lucia's room, he confided, "I think the girl is going to do well. She's making great progress."

As Maggie and Dr. Schambaugh walked back they arrived to the sound of Lucia's coughs as she attempted to dislodge her breathing tube. The anesthesiologist was there, preparing to remove the offending apparatus. With a hearty gag, Lucia's throat muscles expelled the tube, and her eyes opened slightly, as she squinted at those surrounding her. The anesthesiologist held oxygen over her face while suctioning her, studying her to insure that she wasn't aspirating her own saliva into her lungs.

As the drug continued to dissipate from her system, Lucia became more alert. Finally, she sputtered and opened her eyes wide, taking in her surroundings. After a moment, her darting eyes settled on Morgan, and her panic swiftly subsided. Morgan understood her confusion and worked to assure her. "It's okay, Lucia. You're not in trouble. We just want to make sure you're okay."

Lucia evidently felt comfort in the presence of the mother of her best friend. She stared mutely for several moments as expressions chased across her face. Finally, she asked in a raspy voice, "Where's my mom? Is she okay?" Tears were beginning to form in her eyes as she became increasingly frantic.

Morgan rubbed her leg soothingly. "Your mom is fine right now. They have her admitted for observation, but I'm sure she'll be here as soon as she is released."

With a look of concentration, Lucia tested her voice further, saying slowly, "So they didn't get her?" The look on Morgan's face appeared to convince Lucia that her mom was safe, but she soon became guarded once again, and it was blatantly obvious to the adults in the room that she was holding something back.

Quickly making a decision, Morgan requested, "Can I have a minute alone with her? We need to talk."

Sensing the importance of the information that Lucia withheld, the other occupants filed out of the room, but not before the anesthesiologist demanded, "You must hit the emergency light right away if she has trouble breathing. I'll be right out here at the desk to watch her just in case."

Morgan nodded her understanding, taking a seat on the bed next to Lucia. When the child looked to her with those puppy dog eyes, tears on the brink of escaping, Morgan had to fight her own tears and clear her throat before continuing. "Lucia, I don't know what you remember about when I found you, but when I got to your house you were out and your mom was out." She paused for a moment, gauging the child's reaction tentatively. "And then when I was in your room checking on you, a man showed up."

The alarm she saw in Lucia's eyes was evident, and it told Morgan that the child had an idea regarding the identity of the madman. When her face shut down, expression blanking, Morgan entreated her, "Lucia, listen to me." She waited until she saw the whites of her eyes before continuing. When she was sure she had her attention, she explained, "I was there when he showed up. He was going to kill me... you have to tell me who he is."

Lucia swallowed audibly while Morgan sat, never breaking eye contact, quietly and patiently awaiting her answer. Finally, as though talking to herself, the girl sniffed and said, "He was coming for me like he promised."

After making this admission, she glanced tentatively at Morgan, obviously trying to ascertain what the older woman knew. Now that she had revealed her knowledge of the man, Lucia apparently felt she had no other alternative but to confess. "I'm so sorry, Morgan," she spluttered, a volley of tears gliding down her cheeks and spilling onto her hospital gown.

After sniffling and wiping the mess from her face, the girl explained, "I didn't mean for anyone to get hurt, but it just got...got...out of control. I was handling it myself for a minute but then things got bad and I couldn't handle it anymore."

Morgan studied the child's weeping eyes, her thoughts whirling. *What was out of hand? What was out of control?* While still processing the new information, the child confided, "He wanted too much from me...way too much and more than I was comfortable giving him."

Her expression was plaintive, begging Morgan to understand her plight. With tears in her throat, she entreated, "Please don't hate me, Morgan, and don't think I'm a whore." All of her reserves spent, Lucia's emotional dam broke, and she started bawling.

Morgan's heart ached for the girl, demanding that she comfort the crying adolescent. She pulled her in for an embrace, supporting her as she emphatically

considering the question, Morgan continued, "Do you believe that I have your best interests at heart?"

When the girl nodded, Morgan knew with certainty that she was making progress with Lucia, and she pressed on. "I promised my daughter, your best friend, that I would take care of you, Lucia, and I want desperately not to break that promise to her. Please help me to keep it. Tell me what has happened so that I can protect you."

Tears began to fall again, and Lucia seemed resigned to disclosing the ordeal that had led to her current predicament. "I first met him that night at the party…the one you caught me and Stacia at. He seemed so charming, and he was older. And I thought he liked me."

The tears came faster as she admitted, "I just wanted him to like me. Girls at school who have older boyfriends are, like, way more popular. I just thought since he liked me, maybe something good could happen for a change." Morgan handed her a tissue before wrapping her arms around the sobbing child, pulling her in for a soft embrace.

When her shaking subsided, Morgan pulled back and studied the girl. Judging her ready, she prompted Lucia to continue by telling her, "Okay, so you met this guy at that party. Can you tell me what he was doing at your house yesterday?" At her inquiry, Lucia became guarded again, so Morgan cajoled, "You may as well tell me, dear. The guy... what did you say his name was?" She waited for a response patiently, allowing Lucia time to process and choose her words.

After what seemed like forever, Lucia began to recount her trauma. "He called himself Big D, and he's rich. He promised that he would rescue me...take me away from everything. I guess I was being stupid, but I believed him. I thought he loved me."

Morgan listened and remained silent, giving the girl time to collect her thoughts. When she stayed quiet, Morgan prompted, "So what happened Lucia? Why were you so out of it, and why did you take ecstasy?"

Lucia's head snapped up, realizing how much Morgan knew. Sighing, she finally decided to tell the rest. "He wanted me to take it so I would enjoy it more." Seeing the confused look on Morgan's face, she elaborated. "He wanted me to do some things for him. He told me if I really loved him, I would, and he would show me how much he loved me by not being jealous when the other men..."

Morgan could sense the child's internal conflict as the emotions played across her face, the tears falling slowly. Suddenly, Lucia collapsed under the weight of those emotions, a deep moan escaping her throat and her shoulders sagging as sobs racked her body.

When the fit had passed, the little girl rubbed her face, mustering the courage to continue. "He said they were gonna kill him and he needed to make a quick five grand. How could I be so stupid? He was gonna sale me to... to..." Her face contorted in agony as she remembered the conversation with the now-dead man. Another wail escaped before she could contain it, and she buried her face in her hands, weeping into her palms until her misery was momentarily spent.

Morgan worked to process the new information. As she began to grasp the depravity of the situation, her heart sank, and she could feel bile working its way into her throat. She swallowed several times to keep herself from gagging. This girl...her daughter's best friend...her tale was sickening. Looking up, however, Morgan found all thoughts and emotions erased aside from an aching, heartfelt desire to comfort the child that looked so small in the hospital bed.

When Lucia looked up and met her eyes, she looked so utterly forlorn. Morgan pulled her in for a hearty hug. When the girl settled against her shoulder, sobbing and seeming to hold on for dear life, Morgan knew she had made the right decision.

The two embraced until the child's weeping subsided. Morgan pulled back and grasped her chin lightly, forcing Lucia to see her face and listen to her words. "Listen to me, Lucia." She paused for a moment to ascertain that she had her full attention. Satisfied, she released her chin and told her, "I don't know who that fucking creep was, but what he proposed was wrong." When she saw Lucia's instinct to defend the dead man, she hurried to continue. "No, Lucia, you can't do that. I met him very briefly at your house when I found you." The child's curiosity was obviously piqued at her words, although almost certainly for the wrong reason.

Morgan's analysis of Lucia's reaction proved correct as she asked, "Was he there to see me? Did he tell you how much he loves me and needs me?" Morgan's heart went out to her, understanding the desperation behind a craving of the basic human need that should've been inherent from birth. She wanted, with every fiber of her being, to be loved and understood, desperately needing validation.

Proceeding with caution, she said, "Lucia, I'm going to tell you this, and I really need you to understand me. I didn't meet this guy, this 'Big D', while you two were together…but I saw him very briefly at your house when I went to check on you. You were close to death and I couldn't wake you…"

She paused for a moment to give the girl a chance to absorb her words before continuing.

"He showed up not long after I got there to check on you. You see, Stacia was worried about you, so she called me. She was frantic with concern. She worried that, since you hadn't shown up to school, there might be something dire going on with you."

Gauging her reaction, Morgan could see that she wasn't far off the mark with her assessment: regardless of what "Big D" had done, Lucia still craved any manner of attention, even to her own detriment. Seeing the emotional damage lurking behind the girl's dark eyes, Morgan persevered in her course of inquiry. "Lucia, as soon as this guy showed up, I knew I had to keep him from you…I had to protect you."

When she saw the child preparing to argue, she preempted her with a look and a gesture of her hand before continuing. "He's dead, Lucia. Dead." The child's swift intake of breath and bereft expression confirmed Morgan's suspicions.

Again cutting off the girl's arguments, Morgan detailed the altercation that had taken place. "I arrived at your house thinking that Stacia was being overly worried about you. But what I found proved that she was correct, and I'm glad that she sent me there to check on your and your mom's welfare."

At the mention of her mother, a newfound sense of concern crossed the child's face. Before Morgan could continue, Lucia interrupted by demanding, "How's my mom? Did he hurt her?"

Morgan was hesitant to further upset the already distraught girl, but she couldn't hold the information back from the child. "She's alive. He didn't hurt her, but she's in bad shape. Probably from the medicine she has been chronically high on. Her liver has taken a hit from it, but her doctors think that, if she lays off of the hard stuff, she'll make a full recovery." Morgan could see the relief flash across her face, but her expression quickly dampened as she sorrowfully remembered that Big D, the man who she believed had loved her, was now gone.

Morgan decided that swift action was required to convince the girl that the creep, under a guise of caring, would only have hurt her. "So what I was saying, Lucia…before we started talking about your mom. This guy…this Big D…he came in not long after I got there and was yelling out. I'm guessing for you, though he was saying 'Snow White'." A look of recognition crossed her adolescent face, and Morgan chose to dig for more details. "Is there a reason he called you that, Lucia?"

The child looked uncertain for a moment. "He said I was beautiful like Snow White…you know, because I'm so pale and all. He also said that giving me a fake name would protect me better once I started being with all the men." Morgan was still shocked at the prospect of the little girl being sold for sex, as if she were a commodity, no more than cattle.

After swallowing the bile that threatened to rise, she asked Lucia the question that had been bothering her. "Can you tell me more about the valium and the ecstasy?" She could see the obvious guilt in Lucia's expression, and quickly worked to soften the blow. "I just wondered, because the ecstasy was the reason they had to keep you in a coma."

After swallowing heavily, she answered the question of the hour, stating, "It's so stupid. I mean, really. I don't know what the hell I was thinking. Big D gave me the ecstasy so that I would enjoy it…or at least so it wouldn't hurt so badly when he gave me to the men. So I took it that afternoon, then waited. I don't know why, but it didn't seem to work. After like an hour I knew I had to do something, cuz I knew he would be there to get me soon. So I took a couple of my mom's valium to try to make it work faster and stronger. Right after I ate the valium, I could feel it starting to kick in. Not long after that, it really hit me, and I guess I passed out. I don't remember anything after that other than waking up here."

The child suddenly yawned widely, and Morgan could see that the questions had depleted her already meager reserves, exhausting her. She decided to step out of the room to let her rest. Looking up as she rose from Lucia's bed, she suddenly noticed a man hovering at the door. As she registered his presence, he entered the room, introducing himself as one of the sex crimes detectives for the Oklahoma City police department. Cordially, he asked for Lucia's permission to sit down next to her.

Lucia gave a slight nod, but then timidly asked, "Can Morgan stay while I talk to you?"

The detective looked sympathetically at her while shaking his head and saying, "I'm so sorry, Lucia, but this kind of interview has to be done one on one. Would it be okay with you if I ask you some questions with your friend right outside? Then, if you need to take a break, I'll step out and she can come back in."

The little girl raised her arms toward Morgan, who immediately leaned down to embrace her. "I'll be right out here, Loosh. Just say the word, and I'll come back in." Straightening herself, she looked down at the detective and asked, "Don't you need parental permission for this?" Instead of answering, he requested, "Can I speak to you outside for a moment?" She blinked in surprise, but then walked outside with him.

Once in the hallway, he studied her face for a moment before quietly asking, "How well do you know the girl and her mom?" Taken aback yet again, Morgan searched her brain for the answer to his very basic question. After a moment, she informed him, "Let's see…she was five when she and Stacia were in kindergarten together…so about ten years."

Relief flashed briefly across his face, and he explained, "So here's the thing. Due to the living conditions, and the child's state…as well as the mother's mental and physical state…she's been placed in DHS custody. Unless a family member comes forward, she will be going into foster care when she leaves the hospital." He allowed the information to sink in before continuing, "So in answer to your question, her case worker has given me permission to interview the child."

Morgan place her hand over her heart as she heard the news. Though she couldn't say that it was a bad idea to remove Lucia from her mother's care, her heart still went out to both mother and child in this horrible situation.

Before considering further, she piped up, "She can stay with me." She spoke rapidly, surprising even herself with her offer as the words just popped out of her mouth. Regardless, she would never have turned her daughter's best friend away.

Hearing her statement, the detective visibly relaxed. He quickly detailed the necessary hurdles involved in bringing about her proposed arrangement. As he explained the ins and outs of the child welfare system, John approached, and her lover began a slow massage of her neck and shoulders. To Morgan's surprise, his presence calmed her, and his touch brought her a sense of peace. Maggie joined them as well, and Morgan deeply appreciated the support her best friend offered.

His explanation finished, the officer went into the ICU room to begin his interview. Morgan moved to the door, ready to be available should any issues arise. While she waited, John continued his massage, accentuating his handiwork with brief kisses on her neck and shoulders. Morgan closed her eyes, absorbing the feel of his strong hands as she reviewed her conversation with Lucia. When she recalled the details of the girl's ordeal, she struggled not to vomit, forcing herself to take deep and very necessary breaths.

Chapter Ten

When Patrick finally returned to their hotel room, Jasmine was in the shower. Conveniently, this gave him time to prepare their luscious meal. After unpacking the groceries, he quickly went to work sorting and separating.

He'd always enjoyed surprising Jasmine with new activities involving food…creative, sexually pleasurable activities. Smiling to himself, he inventoried the treasures he had found during his shopping spree that morning. He knew that his Jasmine- the love of his life- would immensely enjoy what he planned to do to her.

When Jasmine emerged from the steamy bathroom, their hotel room had been transformed. Her eyes roamed across the room, obviously appreciating the changes he had busily executed during her cleansing shower. For a moment, her expression darkened, and she looked as if she wanted to say something; however, her face brightened again almost immediately as she smiled in anticipation.

As she stepped from the bathroom, Patrick grabbed her from behind and pulled her against him. She looked with gratitude upon the dozens of candles and flowers he had placed, the evidence of his desire to please her. As she took it all in, she felt his rock-hard erection pressing against her back, and a deep moan emanated from her throat. Without restraint, she reached behind herself and took him into her hand, beginning to stroke him. Her delight at finding him unclothed was evident, as she continued to grope him, enjoying her full access to his velvety skin fisted in her palm.

The breath hissed from his mouth in utter satisfaction, and she began to turn, obviously wanting to see his nude body as well as feel it. "No my little love," he said determinedly. "This time it's for you." He accentuated his words by first removing her towel, and then palming her breasts while he fondled her nipples. She rocked back and forth on unsteady legs as he touched her, and he pressed his erection more firmly against her lower back.

"That's right my beloved. Feel my touch. Know that I will give you what it is you crave." As he whispered to her, his hand made its way lazily down the front of her body and nestled over her heated core, resting there. He could feel her…already wet for him. It was just the way he loved her to be, and he was immensely satisfied that his seed was already leaking onto her back; as though he was marking her.

Her head thrown back, Jasmine moaned against his cheek. Patrick moved with her toward the bed, determined to have his way with her. As her body touched the mattress, he parted her thighs with his hands and immediately went to work with his tongue. Her hips bucked, causing her to be more firmly affixed to his mouth, and he savored her flavor as he reminded himself of his other plans for her. He couldn't fully take her quite yet. With a last swipe of his tongue, he pushed away from her. He reached for the berries on the bedside table, looking down at her with an anticipatory grin.

When Jasmine saw the fruit, her smile told Patrick that he had chosen wisely. Then she spied the whipped cream. Her mouth watered and she licked her lips and exclaimed, "Oh Patrick, I'm starving! The strawberries look delicious."

His lips curling in a dark smile, he informed her, "But these are not for you, my sweet. I will be the one eating them, as I eat you." His plan evidently succeeded in turning her on, as her hips immediately bucked, causing her pelvis to push against his thigh. "That's right, *ma shearc*. Whipped cream and strawberries will be sweeter when I eat them out of you."

He wasted no time, quickly inserting the tip of the can of whipped cream into her. He pressed, causing it to spew its frothy contents into her feminine core, filling her up. "It's so cold, my love!" she exclaimed with a high pitched giggle, the cream beginning to squeeze slowly out of her. In answer, he told her, "Don't worry, my beauty, you will soon be warmed up".

Picking up the plumpest strawberry, he made a show of licking the fruit with his tongue while he watched her through hooded eyes. Her answering moans were music to his ears and he couldn't resist tasting her for one moment longer. As he plunged the berry into her feminine channel, her body also plunged toward his hand, assisting him with the placement of the fruit. When he had it where he wanted it, he brought his lips to her and lapped, causing her to moan and move into his mouth.

Their erotic dance continued, Jasmine's hands fisting in his hair as her hips bucked wildly. When Patrick managed to suck the strawberry out of her, he held it in his teeth and brought it to her mouth. As she accepted his offering, his fingers made their way inside her, scooping out the excess cream. Taking possession of her mouth, he dipped his tongue hungrily while his fingers simultaneously dipped into her cream-coated sheath.

As their kiss continued, she became more frantic, her need to find release palpable. Not yet ready to give her what she so desperately wanted, he brought his fingers to his mouth and sucked, tasting her flavor mixed with the whipped cream. His fingers darted into her once more as he brought his lips to hers. As the kiss ended, he replaced his mouth with his fingers, passionately coaxing, "See how delicious you taste, Jasmine…it is why I canna get enough of you."

As his words encouraged her, she hungrily lapped the sweet cream from his fingers. Watching in fascination as her tongue worked him, he could no longer resist the need to be inside her. He mounted her, parting her thighs with his body before entering her with a force that had his balls slapping against her. With each thrust, their pleasure built, Jasmine crying out his name. When she orgasmed, he was rewarded as her slippery channel gripped him, causing his own glorious release to spew into her.

Patrick collapsed on top of her, but remained inside. Turning his face into her neck, he inhaled the clean scent of her skin while Jasmine rubbed his back, caressing him in circles. They lay this way, lost in breathing each other in, until the silence was broken by a knock at the door.

Patrick lifted his face and yelled, "What is it?" Turning to Jasmine, he muttered under his breath, "Bloody bastards disturbing our lovemaking."

The voice coming through the door was Shannon's. "It's checkout time, mate."

Patrick looked down at Jasmine's face, and he knew that he wasn't ready to leave the solace of her body; especially not with an eight hour drive ahead of them. "Late checkout, mate!" he yelled to his friend.

Gazing down at his lover, he reached for her mouth, capturing it with his own. He pulled on her lower lip slightly as she began moving again, bringing him deeper inside of her. "Mmmmm, my love, ye taste so delicious," he mumbled, their tongues intertwining.

As he professed his love, her hands lovingly stroked his cheeks, pulling him closer so that she could kiss him more firmly. When his erection stiffened inside of her, she lifted her torso and pushed him to the side; she obviously wanted to take control.

Complying, he felt her climb atop him. He looked up to see her beautiful face gazing down at his. Her long blonde hair fell like silk curtains, tickling the sensitive skin of his forehead and cheeks. As she rode him, he studied her face, exuding his adoration of her. She seemed to mirror those feelings of devotion with the intensity of her lovemaking. While her hips rocked back and forth, his hands found their way to her breasts, where he rolled her nipples in his fingertips.

A series of moans escaped her mouth, and she began to move more quickly. She rode him leisurely, and while the friction between them was terribly delicious, it was not the vigorous momentum they experienced when he thrust himself into her. Jasmine obviously wanted more, and Patrick felt her thighs tighten, as if aching under the strain as she likely found it difficult to sustain the pace.

Patrick sensed her plight, and in one fluid motion picked her up and flipped her, so that he remained inside of her while landing on top of her. Jasmine beamed with elation at having been flipped so effortlessly…and from the sensation of him so thickly aroused inside of her.

As the pressure and friction built for them both, Patrick increased his pace. Though he could feel her tired muscles tremble beneath him, she obviously took pleasure in the friction he was creating, lifting herself to meet him with each thrust. At the moment when it seemed that the pleasure could climb no higher, they orgasmed together. Wrapped around each other, they lay still to catch their breath.

When they finally managed to regulate their respirations, Patrick propped himself onto his elbows, looking down at her face. "I have a confession to make my love."

Jasmine had been thoroughly enjoying the experience with her lover; however, her heart jumped into her throat, while her biggest fear jumped to the forefront of her brain. She knew he had likely been with someone else during the time he was away from her. The thought nearly brought her to tears, and she considered her own recent transgressions with John. As the unbearable pain threatened to cripple her, she considered that she may not be able to ever tell him of her indiscretions; she couldn't stomach the idea of causing him the same kind of hurt that she felt at that very moment.

She knew her face was transparent when he stroked it tenderly and said, "It's nothing like that, love. For me, no other woman could ever compare to you, so I would never think to be with another. You can count on that my dear one." When she could finally breathe again, he kissed her lips and continued, "I think…" He seemed to be having difficulty with his confession.

Though Jasmine was calmer than before, his internal conflict made her nervous. "Just say it, my beloved. Whatever you are going to say can't possibly be worse than what I am imagining." She couldn't stop the tears that were in her voice, and she braced herself for whatever he would reveal.

"Okay. I'm sorry. You're right." He took a deep breath and then blurted out, "I think Callie is mine and not John's."

The relief she felt was immediate and overwhelming, and she exhaled loudly, kissing her man deeply and thoroughly. When they finally came up for air, she smiled at his confusion. "We…that is, John and I…just recently figured that out. It was yesterday in fact."

She waited for his reaction…and was elated to see the overly large smile that spread across his face. "So she's mine then? John won't fight me over her?" His question seemed to make the world stop turning. Jasmine was fearful for a moment of what might happen if John did, in fact, choose to fight them.

Before she could hyperventilate, Patrick smoothed her hair back from her face and assured her, "Don't worry, my sweet. We will work it out, one way or the other. I won't let him hurt you…I promise." She snuggled into his chest, knowing beyond all doubt that she and Patrick were perfect together. He had always been able to calm her with the simplest of touches and the softest of words. As he withdrew from her and started the process of packing up their things, she closed her eyes and relished the feel of her body after having been so thoroughly loved.

****

As Morgan left the hospital, she reviewed the long list of things she needed to do in order to take Lucia home with her. As she drove away, her thoughts were interrupted when her phone began to buzz; checking the caller ID on the dashboard, she saw that the call was from her daughter. Mentally kicking herself for not having phoned with an update sooner, Morgan hit the button on her steering wheel that answered the phone.

Before her daughter could begin her frantic questions, Morgan beat her to it by announcing, "She's going to be fine, Stacia. And by the way, she is going to be staying with us for a while…if I can get it all worked out."

Morgan was thankful when that tidbit of information halted further queries about Lucia's wellbeing…or the cause of her hospitalization. Stacia rambled for thirty minutes about how excited she was; finally, Morgan had to cut her off to end the phone call. Stopping the car, she realized where she had driven herself.

Looking up at the Irish cottage-like house, she examined the emotions and events of the past twenty-four hours. She was so tired that she wanted nothing more than to lay her head down and sleep for a few weeks; but she didn't feel right about invading John's space while he wasn't even there.

Luckily, her rambling thoughts halted abruptly when John's Lexus pulled into the driveway behind her. Seeing his headlights, she stepped out of her car and walked the few feet to his driver's side window. Though she was irritated with herself for her errant behavior, John's smile was invigorating, and she was happy to see that he was just as excited to see her.

"Did you reconsider the offer, my little lamb?" The way he looked and smiled at her made her panties wet, and for a split second, she thought that moving in with him wouldn't be such a bad idea. However, reality quickly returned, and she dismissed the thought as crazy. However, that didn't stop her from leaning over and kissing him as she reached through the window to grab his crotch.

Both hot and aroused, she lifted her head and whispered in his ear, "I couldn't get enough of you, so I had to come get a taste of what I will be missing once everyone returns."

The intensity of his hungry stare practically screamed that John was close to losing control… she was unsure of his intentions when he opened the driver's side door. Closing the door behind him, he stood before her, looking down at her as if studying her face. "That was a dangerous thing to do, my love. We are not yet in the house, and I don't know if I can keep myself from taking you right here." As she gazed up at him, she thought of how imposing he looked. Her mind invoked images of him provoked, doing what was necessary to protect his family.

As his erection pushed against her belly, she could feel her panties becoming wet all over again. Suddenly, she couldn't wait to get inside the house, needing him inside of her. It would not do to be caught in the driveway or the yard. Turning around abruptly, she took off at a sprint toward the front door, hoping to make it in before John lost control completely.

Quick on the uptake, John caught up to her after five and a half steps. Before she realized what was happening, John had swung her over his shoulder as if she was weightless, continuing to run with her toward their destination.

Once they reached the door, he set her down; finally, she thought they were safe. However, as John began fumbling for the code to unlock the door, his hands began roaming over her body, practically undressing her on the porch. He ripped her panties away and dipped his fingers inside of her. With the first insertion, his breath hissed out and he exclaimed, "Fuck, Morgan! You're so hot and wet for me." As he sought to bring his fingers to his mouth, his hand became hooked in her skirt; when he pulled his hand away he inadvertently exposed her, and she could feel the icy February draft, against her bare flesh.

Abruptly, John turned her around, facing the door, and he managed to whisper the code to her through gritted teeth. As she hastily punched in the numbers, she could hear his zipper. As she pushed the door open, he entered her with a force.

While still partially on the front porch, she felt shy for a split second, but the pleasure was so great that she could do nothing but hold onto his hands where they gripped her hips. After thrusting inside of her several more times, he finally managed to slam the door shut behind them. Unable to hold back further, he leaned her over the table in the home's entryway and pounded into her. The thought briefly occurred to Morgan that she couldn't even recall moving further into the house; let alone making it all the way into the entryway.

With the table supporting her weight, he held her hands over her head with one hand and began roaming her body with his other hand. He fondled her between her legs, moving upward to feel her soft breasts. As her orgasm tore through her, she yelled out his name, and his own orgasm propelled from him with a force to rival any gunshot.

For what seemed like forever, they stood together, John draped across her. Finally, she turned her face to look up at him. Smiling, she extracted his hand from where it rested on her ribs, suckling his middle finger into her mouth. As she increased the suction, his erection grew harder inside of her. However, it was obvious that he wanted desperately to take her somewhere other than the entryway of his home.

Suddenly, extracting his hand and moving it to her hip, he picked her up. Placing her feet on top of his, he walked with her to the stairs. As she looked up, she wondered if he would stay inside her as they ascended the grand staircase.

The ascent was slow going, but extremely pleasurable for them both. When they arrived at the middle landing, he stopped and turned her to the banister, beginning to piston into her while his fingers traced circular caresses on her nipples. She came immediately, rewarding him with a hot wet release. She could just make out his words when his voice exclaimed, "Oh Morgan, you make it impossible for me to control myself!" As he bit out the last of his proclamation through gritted teeth, he came, filling her with his essence. He stopped to rest over her again, but then continued his ascent while still inside of her. Gripping her hips, he partially carried her and partially walked her up the stairs.

Finally arriving at their destination, Morgan was surprised and excited as he lay her down on the bed. She was splayed out, naked and open for his hungry eyes. He withdrew from her in order to settle her onto the bed, but he quickly re-entered her, and for both of them it was heaven; he was home when he was lodged within her core, and she knew that no other lover would ever compare to him, or even come close for that matter.

Moving back and forth, he took it slow this time, drawing it out for both of them. Every so often, he accentuated a thrust with a kiss of her chin or a light nip of her earlobe. His hips undulated as he moved into her, taking great pleasure in the ride he was providing. When he leaned in for his next kiss, she captured his face in her hands, bringing him to her mouth. She held him there. They remained joined, making love with their bodies and their mouths.

Finally, the pleasure becoming too much, he broke off the kiss, leaving them both breathless. As he increased the pace, he moved a pillow under her hips, angling her pelvis toward him so that he could go deeper. As the intensity of this new position gripped them in its vice, it took scant few seconds before they orgasmed together. Pushing the pillow out from beneath her, John lay next to her and cradled her, his knee over her legs and her head pulled close to his face.

As they lay together, peacefully inhaling the scent of their passion, he kissed her chin and cheeks with light caresses of his lips. She moved into his embrace, losing herself in a breathy kiss, after which they lay staring into each other's eyes. "I cannot get enough of you," he professed, gazing at her lovingly.

"Mmmmm, John," she responded throatily. "Your words are music to my ears. I would never think that I could fall so quickly for you. I love you so much. It's like an impossible, delicious dream come true."

She snuggled further into the cradle of his body, and they held each other tenderly as they both dozed off into oblivion.

Chapter Eleven

When her cell phone rang, Morgan woke with a start. Looking at the time, she was surprised to realize that a full five hours had passed while she slept with John. Glancing at her phone, she noted from the caller ID that it was her father; she fumbled with the phone as she hurried to answer, alarmed that he was calling her at such a late hour.

"Daddy? Is everything okay?" she asked.

To her relief, he assured her that everything was fine, and then continued by explaining that they would have to delay their return from Florida because of a blizzard that was scheduled to move through the Midwest over the next several days.

Hanging up the phone several moments later, she turned to John and couldn't help her smile or the blush that crept up her face. John was wearing her panties on his face, and she could hear a faint sniffing as the thin fabric ballooned in and out with his breathing. Finally noticing, he quickly ripped the undergarment from his face, reaching for her with a guilty grin. "If I can't taste you now, my sweet, because you are on the phone, then I must smell your flavor somehow." His actions, along with his thick Irish accent, had her wet, and as he pulled her on top of him, she ground her bottom into his erection.

Nipping her ear softly, he whispered, "I love it when I feel this rubbing up against me." She felt his fingers pinch her butt cheek as his words caressed her. She was prompted to grind against him again as he brought his hand around to fondle her. She turned her face to him, answering, "I love it when I feel you touching me like this." She kissed his mouth as she turned her body to face his.

Their kiss deepening, he moved to blanket her with his body, placing himself between her thighs. She felt even more turned on as he nibbled her bottom lip, sucking it gently into his mouth. He was stoking her passion in exactly the way she liked, and she betrayed this fact with her rapid breaths. However, he appeared to have overwhelming needs of his own as he licked his lips, obviously remembering her panties and his desire to taste her.

He descended her body, placing soft kisses on her breasts and hips. When he arrived at his destination, he hovered over her, looking up to study her face. Then he moved toward her heated core, and her breath escaped in a rush at the anticipation of his touch.

When he took her with his mouth, her hips bucked, and she fisted her hands in his hair, pulling him roughly, affixing herself more firmly to him. His tongue swirled wickedly, quickly bringing her to the verge of orgasm. When she pulled his hair in an attempt at prompting him to mount her, he looked up into her pleading eyes, shaking his head and smiling. She persisted in her heated request, her hips beginning to move frantically. Not ready to relinquish his meal, he brought his forearm over her hips to hold her still while he continued his work. Her eyes became wild, and she begged him, "Please John, I need you inside me!"

He grinned at her, releasing her delicate skin briefly to tease her, and said, "No, my love, I have not had my fill of you. You will have to take the pleasure I am giving you until I am ready." With this, he returned to his luscious meal. She could do nothing but close her eyes and ride the waves of pleasure he was creating, though her hands continued to pull at his hair as her head whipped back and forth on the pillow.

Opening her eyes, Morgan looked down the length of her body, watching John. His tongue continued to lap at her, savoring the sweet cream she emitted for him. She could see his enjoyment as he returned her gaze, watching her face contort in sweet agony, knowing he was the cause. The pressure continued to grow within her, the pleasant building from a steady blaze to a roaring inferno. At last, it appeared John could ignore the same pressure within himself no longer.

Releasing his hold on her, he moved until he was poised before her opening. He then entered her with a force that had her moaning hoarsely and then thrusting herself against him. "Oh…John!" she groaned, as his thrusts became more vigorous. Having already orgasmed multiple times, it was a surprise when she still came over and over while he moved inside of her. With one final thrust, his seed jetted into her, and he finally lay still, breathing heavily on top of her.

They lay together, connected for the longest time, until the breathless silence was broken by John's phone ringing. Still on top of her, he shifted carefully and reached for the phone, answering roughly with a growl, "What?"

As the person on the other line replied, his expression changed, softening as he became thoughtful. After a moment, he answered, "Tonight? How long?" As the information came across, he nodded, grunting an affirmation of understanding, and then hung up the phone. Turning to Morgan, he announced, "My family will return home within the hour."

She swallowed nervously and paused briefly before asking, "Should I go, darling?"

He was startled by her question, and hurried to reassure her, "No way! Don't even consider it. I want you here with me. In front of my family and everyone…Unless you want to go, that is." His voice raised slightly at the end, obviously hoping for a response that she wanted to stay with him; hoping for her support.

"I wouldn't think of leaving, if you want me to stay, John," she assured him.

He kissed her lips slowly and deeply, pulling her against him once more. As much as Morgan wanted to be with him again before the big group showed up, she stopped him, explaining that she needed to call Maggie and check in on Lucia. He nodded his understanding, and she made the call.

When Maggie answered, Morgan immediately heard the distress in her friend's voice. Despite prodding, however, Maggie would discuss only Lucia's care…and plans for Morgan to take Lucia home the next day. Unsatisfied with the inadequate information, Morgan decided to confront her friend, pressing, "What are you upset about? You may as well tell me."

After releasing an audible sigh, Mag explained her most recent difficulties: her power was out from the ice storm, and she generally was having a difficult time being alone. Thinking about Maggie's house- *the* house where Maggie's mother had just essentially died- Morgan decided that it just wouldn't do for her best friend to be stuck there. "Just a sec, Mags," she told her.

Turning to John, Morgan placed the phone against her chest. "John, I hate to ask, but do you mind if Maggie spends the night here tonight? She's alone at her house and her power's out."

John changed course in his stroll across the room, walking over to her. Taking her face in his hands, he expressed tenderly, "My love, you are welcome here anytime, and so are your friends and loved ones. Think of my home as yours…because where you are is home to me."

Morgan was so touched by both his words and his generosity. For him to be so welcoming to her- despite her recent refusal to live with him- made her heart melt, and she fell in love with him all over again. Though she knew her friend was waiting for an answer, she continued to hold the receiver against her chest for a few minutes more, followed immediately by a heated embrace. When their passion was momentarily spent, she whispered to him, "I love you right now more than words can express." He smiled at her sentiment, and then gestured toward the phone, which had slipped to her abdomen.

Remembering her best friend at last, she lifted the phone to her ear and announced, "Hey Mags, sorry about that." She sounded breathless to her own ears and had to swallow before continuing. "I'm staying at John's tonight. Why don't you head up here and spend the night? It'll be fun…like a slumber party." Maggie took a bit of convincing, requiring several assurances that she wouldn't be imposing. In the end, Maggie's loneliness won out, and Morgan smiled as her best friend agreed to spend the night. After giving directions to the home, Morgan hung up.

Emerging from the master suite a short time later, Morgan looked around for John. Not sensing his presence in the rooms around her, she proceeded downstairs, listening for any sound as she searched for him. A delicious aroma assailed her as she approached the kitchen, and upon entering, she was greeted by a sight that she would never have expected: John was busying himself at the stove, stirring a huge pot. She watched him for a moment, fascinated by the sight of him as he lost himself in his work.

Finally, he turned around and, noticing her, smiled. "My darling, I'm so glad to make my specialty for you." He gestured to the enormous pot, inviting her to join him. Looking down into the bubbling liquid and breathing in the aroma, she deduced that it was some type of marinara sauce.

John dipped a large spoon into the pot and brought it to his mouth, blowing at the aromatic steam. Testing it with the tip of his tongue, he must have found the temperature to his satisfaction, as he then brought the spoon to her mouth, encouraging her to taste his creation.

Immediately, Morgan decided that it was
the most flavorful marinara she had ever tasted.
"Mmmmm," she complimented, as John watched her
work the spoon with her tongue. "It is my pleasure to
care for you, my love," he told her in a husky whisper.

When he nipped her earlobe, she had to resist
the temptation to throw him down right there on the
kitchen floor, reminding herself that Maggie would
be arriving shortly. However, she did wrap her arms
around his neck to kiss him thoroughly on the lips.
"I love the way you care for me, John," she told him,
snuggling into his neck. They stood quietly together,
breathing each other in, until the doorbell rang.

"Get the door, will you love, so I can work on
my masterpiece," John requested. She gladly obliged,
and was so overjoyed that she practically skipped.

After opening the door wide, she threw
her arms around a stunned Maggie, taking her by
surprise. "I'm so glad you're here, Mags! It'll be like
old times."

Mag sputtered for a moment, and then
exclaimed, "Holy moly, Morgan, you didn't say this
guy was loaded! What does he do for work, own an
oil company?"

Morgan laughed good-naturedly at her best
friend's shock...but was then taken aback realizing
that she wasn't, in fact, sure what John did for a

living. Shrugging her shoulders, she led Maggie to the kitchen, telling her, "You know, I'm not really sure. I guess we should ask him."

When the two ladies entered the kitchen, John looked up from a second over-large pot, setting down the large wooden spoon. Walking up to them, he gently took Maggie's fingertips in his immense grip, and with a slight bow he kissed her hand, saying, "Welcome to my home, dear. You are always welcome here," with a slight bow and a kiss on her hand that he had taken into his. Morgan was again reminded of how charming he could be; recalling how both his manners and his accent were reminiscent of an old world gentleman, she blushed slightly.

However, her blush was nothing compared to Mag's glowing cheeks and neck. When the silence continued for a moment too long, she stammered, "Thank you, John. You're so very…gracious." He gave a slight nod, accepting her compliment, and then walked over to the kitchen's center island. Pulling out two barstools for them, he gestured and said, "Please, have a seat," before going back to his pots.

After seating herself, Morgan asked him, "John, I was wondering…that is." He looked up at her, patiently awaiting her query. When she still seemed hesitant, he prompted her, saying, "My love, you can ask me anything. There is nothing to be nervous about, especially not with your best friend here." With his assurance, Morgan had the courage to continue, and asked, "John, I just realized that I don't know what it is that you do for work. Would you mind telling me?"

John's lips curved up slightly with amusement, and after clearing his throat he looked pointedly at Maggie, indicating the obvious source of his lover's curiosity. Explaining for Mag's benefit, he began, "In my country, Ireland, we are from a very wealthy family. You might say we are like royalty there, although Ireland isn't a monarchy. So, you see, we come from what you Americans call 'old money'."

While John talked of his homeland, his accent thickened somewhat, and Morgan decided that she could listen to him speak for hours. As he continued, he took Morgan's hands in his, placing kisses on the backs of each knuckle before tucking stray strands of hair behind her ears. "Though my family does not officially rule the native Irish, we still hold a great deal of power over many who live there. They listen to us and we are good to them."

Moving behind Morgan, he began to massage her shoulders and neck in tight circles. She stifled her moan of pleasure as he continued talking, addressing the subject of his current occupation. "Since moving to America, I have been quite fortunate in my business ventures. I came to the decision that I wanted to live here for a period of time, and allotted myself a set amount of the family's money to invest before I would call it quits and move back home. In the five years since moving here, I have more than quadrupled my original investment. It seems I have a gift when it comes to choosing what to invest in."

The two ladies quietly absorbed the information, but finally Morgan's curiosity got the better of her. "But why did you move here in the first place, John? What made you want a change from your homeland?"

John poured wine, depositing a glass in front of each of them, and answered, "Let's see. My mother needed a change in scenery…the damp weather there seemed to keep her constantly under the weather. And my wife…well, she and I both drastically needed to be away from there. The place just held so many unpleasant memories for us.

"So we wanted a new start, and we chose Oklahoma City because it has such a unique position in the country. And its economy is booming at this time, despite so many other cities being in dire straits. In truth, I am very glad we chose to move here. Had we not, I would not have met this lovely creature that consumes my every waking moment." The last of his statement was spoken as he looked intently into Morgan's eyes. Her answering blush spread from forehead to belly button. She felt a great sense of relief as John moved to mask her blush, standing between her thighs and capturing her mouth, suckling her bottom lip.

John continued to hold her in his arms for a few blissful moments, and Morgan drifted, enjoying his warmth and his scent…until Maggie cleared her throat, reminding the couple that a guest was still in the room with them. Releasing her, John suggested amiably, "Why don't you show our guest around the house and help her get settled in? The best place for her will be the room past the nursery." Seeing Morgan's confusion, he remembered that she hadn't seen the entire house since the renovations, and he quickly explained, "Take a left from the stairs and go to the third room on the right." As the two friends exited via the same door through which they had entered, Morgan could see John returning to the stove to stir the contents of both pots.

Once they were out of ear shot, Maggie stopped her and exclaimed, "Oh my God, Morg! Is it always like that with you two?" Evidently seeing Morgan's confusion, she prompted, "I mean the way he kissed you, and the things he said…it's like he worships you. Is he always like that?"

Morgan could feel her blush returning, and she wasted no time in confirming her best friend's suspicions as she nodded, grinning from ear to ear. "He is so…intense," she started. She hugged herself around the waist for a moment, smiling like a school girl, before finishing, "I am so in love, Mags. I never thought this kind of thing would happen to me. But I love him so much already, and we are so…into each other." She had to search for the right words in order to get anywhere close to describing her feelings for him.

Glancing toward her friend, Morgan noticed the expression- unconscious certainly- that crossed Maggie's face; an expression that could only be called jealousy. While she knew that Mag was happy to see her so much in love, Morgan also knew that her friend had been lonely for so long. Moving closer to her friend, she realized Maggie was preparing to speak, perhaps just searching for the right words to convey her feelings.

The two friends had always been extremely close, and had therefore developed a habit of simply telling each other the truth…no matter how difficult or unpleasant that truth might be. Due to the heartache she sensed coming from Maggie, Morgan's response was one of empathy, and she told her dearest friend, "Oh Mags, I really am blissfully happy. I wish I could find someone like him for you. God knows you deserve it." The two women hugged and then entered the room that John had indicated.

Taking in the room's décor, Morgan immediately understood that the Kennedy's had spared no expense while ensuring the room's comfort. It was decked out with antique furniture, including a four poster bed where thick and decadent curtains hung to the floor.

A massive fireplace adorned the room's one exterior wall, and Morgan could just imagine cozying up by it with a roaring fire...especially considering the current ice storm that the city was enduring. The walls of the room were a deep rich red, and the wood floors were beautiful, and so highly polished that Morgan could almost see her reflection. The room's most noticeable feature, however, was the magnificent Persian rug that took up a good two-thirds of the floor; even without being an antiques dealer, Morgan knew that it must have cost a small fortune.

Maggie, appreciatively admiring the luxurious suite in which she would be sleeping, was impressed and excited. "Wow! This is where I get to stay the night? I don't think I've ever stayed in a hotel room that was even half this fancy!" Morgan broke into laughter at her enthusiasm, sharing her sentiment.

Immediately, they went to work checking the drawers of the room's wardrobe. Satisfied, they proceeded to one of the two doors adorning the walls, excited to investigate the adjoining room. Opening the doors revealed a large bathroom with a décor which left them both speechless. When Maggie walked in behind her, she exclaimed, "O...M...G!" She gestured to the deep-set tub. "I am totally taking a bath in *that* tonight!"

Morgan was deeply impressed that John had gifted her best friend with such a magnificent suite. Wishing to return to the kitchen- and to thank him properly- she turned to Maggie and suggested, "You get settled in. I have got to go thank John for this." As she left the room, she could hear Maggie beginning to fill the bathtub.

When she returned to the kitchen, John was still occupied with the food simmering in the two pots, stirring occasionally. Spotting her, he asked, "Is everything satisfactory for your friend's stay?" In answer, Morgan threw her arms around him and kissed him, plunging her tongue into his mouth.

Coming up for air, the two lovers gazed adoringly at one another, John rubbing her back lightly while she ran her hands over his forearms. Their embrace was abruptly interrupted when John's mother entered the kitchen carrying Deirdre.

"Ma, you're back!" John exclaimed, taking the sleeping child from her arms. "How was the drive?"

"The drive was long and I am cold. Now who is *this*?" she asked as she looked Morgan up and down. Morgan blanched slightly at the older woman's coarse tone, and John's face immediately darkened.

Turning to his mother, his words were clearly delivered as a reprimand. "Mother, this is my girlfriend, Morgan, who I love very much." He spoke the last words in a clipped tone; one that challenged her to continue her rudeness.

When the old woman looked at her again, Morgan saw her expression soften as she said, "I apologize for the rudeness, dear. Long car rides make me a titch upset...especially with the love birds in the front, and the children's endless chattering and crying behind." Holding her arms out, she approached Morgan. "It is very nice to meet ye, dearie. I welcome ya to our home, and I hope ye make me son deliriously happy, as he deserves."

Blushing- as was her habit of late- Morgan stepped into the confines of her arms.

She was completely off guard, and sputtered for a moment; but seeing the pride shining in John's eyes, she regained her composure and told the woman, "Thank you, Brunne. That means a lot to me."

Brunne was apparently taken aback at the fact that Morgan knew her name. An eyebrow raised in inquiry, the older woman asked, "Have we met before?"

Morgan's explanation was interrupted as, through the kitchen doorway, Patrick and Jasmine entered, Callie snuggled peacefully in Patrick's arms. Morgan noticed that Patrick held the child very close to his chest and that his expression was one of fierce pride. During the trip, Jasmine must have told him that the child was his.

Releasing Brunne, Morgan went to Jasmine, hugging her joyfully. "I'm glad you're back safely, Jasmine. How was your trip?"

Jasmine returned the hug, kissing Morgan on the cheek, and then answered, "It was a delightful jaunt, but I'm glad to be home, and I'm glad you're here. This is Patrick." Jasmine beamed at her lover as she made the introduction.

Patrick gave a slight nod, and then in his thick accent stated, "Yes m'love, I have met her. Is this… John's?"

His question ended abruptly when John wrapped his arms around Morgan's waist and stared intently at his brother, announcing, "She is my beloved, Patrick, and I expect you to remember that always." The threat in John's voice was unmistakable, and it caused the hair on the back of Morgan's neck to stand on end.

"You and I need to talk, brother. Man to man." Patrick's voice was very quiet, but he also looked John directly in the eye. Morgan worried that the two would become physical. Patrick handed the sleeping babe to Jasmine, and John released his hold on her.

"My office, brother," John command. Turning to Morgan, he asked in a gentle voice, "My love, will you please keep an eye on the pasta and sauce? It must be stirred quite frequently." After waiting for her answering nod, he kissed her lips softly, hugging her, before following Patrick into his office.

"Those two will be the death of me," Brunne sighed around the sleeping child in her arms. "Oh well, let's let those two blokes work things out. Jasmine, why don't ye join me in putting the children to bed."

Jasmine followed her mother-in-law out of the kitchen, leaving Morgan to the food and her thoughts.

Chapter Twelve

Once the hot water had finally seeped in enough to take some of the cold out of her bones, Maggie dragged herself out of the tub. As she stood, the bathroom door opened. Assuming that it was Morgan, she was shocked when instead a naked man came strolling in. For one frozen moment, the two could only stand and stare at one another, each taking in the stark nudity of the other.

Finally, Maggie bent over and picked up the towel from the side of the tub, never taking her eyes off of the stranger. This seemed to break his trance as, realizing that he too had no clothing on, he quickly grabbed a hand towel from the nearby rack.

When he spoke, his thick Irish accent caused Maggie's already glowing blush to darken to a deeper red. "Lassie, I didna know there was a beautiful…I mean bare naked lady in here. Please forgive me intrusion."

Her attention diverted by the vision standing before her, her foot suddenly slipped as she stepped from the tub, and she felt herself toppling over. In a flash, the man was there to catch her, wrapping his arms around her. She opened her mouth to express gratitude…when *his* foot slipped on the wet floor, and they both went down. As they fell, the man spun, causing her to fall on top of him, his body breaking her fall.

Though her towel acted as a barrier between them, she could feel that he was very much turned on. Unable to ignore the sensation, she glanced down at the place where he pressed into her. His hand instinctively moved to cover his bulge, trying to hide it from her. Looking back up to his face, Maggie gave him a shy smile that clearly stated that she knew exactly what it was that he was attempting to conceal. The situation was not helped by the fact that his erection pushed against her chest; in hiding his erection, he placed his hand very close to her bare breast.

"I...I..." Maggie stuttered. Any words she had meant to say were lost when he pulled her face to his and kissed her on the lips. He was slow and tentative at first, testing her acceptance. When she hungrily returned the kiss, they both began breathing heavily. He then pulled her on top of him and brought her legs around, wrapping them around his waist, his phallus pushing against the entrance of her feminine channel.

Their hands roamed each other's bodies unceasingly. Feeling the intensity of his touch, and frustrated with the barrier that separated them, Maggie removed the towel, pulling the strip of cloth from between their bodies and throwing it into the tub. As soon as the towel was gone, she shifted her hips, bringing him into her, and eliciting a groan. Unable to find purchase on the wet bathroom floor, he stood up, holding her and carrying her over the threshold into the bedroom.

While he focused on not running them into anything, she focused on kissing him. Her lips had roamed over most of his face by the time they arrived at the bed. As he settled her onto the mattress, he remained inside of her, thrusting back and forth and savoring the sounds she made. She moaned loudly as his movements sent zings of pleasure through her.

After suckling her tongue, he pulled back to gaze down upon her naked body. His gaze shifting to her breasts, he leaned forward and took one of her beckoning nipples into his mouth, causing her to cry out. Upon hearing her pleasure, he continued swirling his tongue while pistoning into her, bringing her to orgasm as she moaned into his hair. The throaty moans of her pleasure seemed to have an extreme effect on him, as he suddenly lost control, his climax erupting and leaving them both gloriously and deeply sated.

Supporting himself on his elbows to keep from smashing her, he looked down at her face and smiled. He appeared to genuinely appreciate her beauty, echoing her thankfulness for the luck that had brought him to her room.

She looked up at him and couldn't help but smile back, shyly at first. Soon however, she grinned at him widely, declaring, "I am quite impressed, although taken aback. Would you give me the pleasure of knowing your name, since you have already given me the pleasure of your body?"

Their shared laughter elicited even more giggles, and before either could help it, they were both in tears from their shared merriment. When the man could finally speak again, he shook her hand and introduced himself in his thick Irish brogue.

"Shannon Kelly at ye're service, ma'am."

She took his offered hand as she processed his accent, butterflies taking flight in her stomach. She had to swallow before she could answer him. "Maggie," was all she managed to get out, pointing to herself and feeling like a shy child. Embarrassed by her lack of grace, her blush returned, and she felt foolish.

Responding to her bashfulness, Shannon captured her mouth with his, saving her from any further embarrassment. She took his offering and held him tightly as they kissed. She couldn't remember a time when she had ever been so turned on. Her fingertips moved continuously over his back and neck, and then fisted in his hair.

Suddenly, they were interrupted by a knock at the door. Hurriedly, Shannon moved to cover her with the bedclothes, trying to protect her modesty from prying eyes. His efforts were considerably hindered, however, when the tight tuck of the comforter foiled the attempt.

The door swung open, and Jasmine entered the room, stopping abruptly. "Oh Shannon, I'm…I…," she stuttered, obviously trying to come up with something to mitigate the situation. Giving up, she dropped the bundle of blankets intended for the room and hurried out, slamming the door shut behind her.

Maggie couldn't stifle the giggle that seemed bent on escaping, which in turn brought a fresh volley of laughter from Shannon as well. As the two lay together gazing upon each other, an expression crossing Shannon's face alerted Maggie that the moment was becoming awkward. She rested her hands on the mattress on either side of her, prompting him to move.

After withdrawing from where he was lodged inside her, Shannon stood up and offered his hand. After helping her to regain vertical positioning, he walked to his luggage, unzipping it while he asked, "Shall we go meet everyone then?"

Maggie was surprised by his abrupt change of demeanor, and she felt a spike of rejection at his sudden change; further, she suddenly felt vulnerable. Nodding slightly in his direction, she took her cue and went into the bathroom to dress. She closed the door behind her, effectively shutting him out. Working to process what had just taken place between them, she had to sit on the toilet for a moment to collect her thoughts.

"I'm going downstairs, lass," Shannon's voice announced through the door. She managed to say, "K," in response, deciding that she needed to get it.

Shaking her head at recent events, she left the bathroom. It wasn't like her to be so wanton. Within days after her mother's death, she had been with two different men. Maybe it was the effect of the grief she was experiencing.

Stirring the marinara, Morgan waited tensely for the two brothers to finish their talk...or for violence to erupt. She strained her ears, listening for any telltale signs from John's office. Unfortunately, she could only hear occasional murmurs. Staring into the pot, she was surprised when a man she had not previously met entered the kitchen.

When he saw her, he paused briefly, but then continued his trek while announcing, "Hello Lass, I'm Shannon, Patrick's friend. And ye are?"

Morgan blinked at him before answering, "I'm Morgan, John's girlfriend." The new label of her relationship status tasted foreign on her tongue.

He paused, considering her statement, and then offered his hand. As they shook, he nodded his head to her in a slight bow, offering, "It's a pleasure to make ye're acquaintance."

Morgan could see that he had a nice smile and seemed good-natured. She decided that she liked him, immediately thinking about introducing him to Maggie. Excited to have something to do other than stir the sauce and fret over the brothers, Morgan asked him, "Will you be so kind as to stir this while I go check on something?"

As he stepped up to the stove, taking over, she all but ran out of the kitchen, hurrying to the room where she had left Maggie. Arriving at her destination, she was surprised to see Maggie lying in bed, apparently retiring for the night.

Morgan excitedly told her, "I just met the cutest guy, Maggie! You have to come down so I can introduce you." Mag's cynical smile told Morgan more than words could have. Sitting next to her friend, she exclaimed, "Oh no! Did he hurt you?"

Maggie sat up abruptly, shaking her head in an attempt to keep Morgan from running out and doing something embarrassing. "No, no. He did…something amazing to me," Mag said, smiling shyly.

Morgan studied her face, puzzled for a moment, finally understanding. "Okay, so give me the deets, and don't leave anything out."

When a shadow crossed Maggie's face, Morgan suspected that her friend would not likely tell her much; she was surprised, however, when Maggie admitted, "We did it, Morgan. I'm astonished at myself, but it was really great and it was a lot of fun."

Feeling slightly confused, Morgan patted her friend's leg tentatively and inquired, "Okay, that's great! So what's wrong, Mags?" The shadow returned as Maggie started to close up, and Morgan immediately prompted, "This is me that you're talking to Maggie…your best friend. The one you can share anything with."

Maggie looked up at her for a moment before nodding, apparently coming to a decision. "It's just that…gosh, it's so stupid, Morgan. I'm such an idiot sometimes." Morgan waited quietly and patiently for her friend to collect her thoughts. Finally, she continued, "Well, you know how I've always been so…careful about who I have sex with." Morgan nodded her understanding. Maggie eventually continued, "Well, I think it's because for me I want to save it for someone I love."

Morgan waited for her to say more; looking at Maggie, she was confused at her friend's expression, as the woman apparently expected Morgan's condemnation. Realizing that Maggie had reached the end of her confession, Morgan's heart went out to her, knowing that she had to reassure her. "Maggie, listen to me. There is nothing, and I mean abso-fucking-lutely nothing wrong with you wanting to only have sex with a person you love."

Emphasizing her words to drive the point home, Morgan continued as Maggie took several deep breaths. "Don't get me wrong. I'm not saying that what you did with Shannon was wrong either. You've said so yourself, Mags…sex is a physiological need."

Maggie appeared to absorb Morgan's words, thinking, but she finally shook her head and explained, "It's not that I'm upset that I had sex with him." As she spoke, a fresh blush crept up her neck and a small smile touched her lips. Her eyes had wandered the room as Morgan spoke to her…when making this admission, however, she stared Morgan in the eye. "I loved it, Morg. It was really good. And when it was over…" She stared into space for a moment. "I wanted it to be more, and that's what I don't like."

Understanding dawned on Morgan's face. Seeing that her best friend was close to tears, she leaned forward and wrapped her arms around the distraught woman's shoulders. Maggie allowed herself to be hugged, the embrace comforting for mere moments before the tears began to fall. Morgan silently held her weeping friend; suddenly, Maggie ended the embrace, lifting her head and demanding, "Why am I so fucked up, Morgan? I'm such an idiot. This guy…a complete stranger…has sex with me one time, and I'm falling in love with him. What is wrong with me?"

Grabbing a tissue from the night stand and handing it to Maggie, Morgan assured her, "Listen to me, baby. There is nothing wrong with you. You need to give yourself some credit here." She paused, seeking verification that she had Maggie's full attention. "Think about it, Mags. Your mom just passed away. Lucia, a kid who you know and love is in the hospital after enduring god knows what with the dead guy. And to top it all off, you're not at home in familiar surroundings.

"Give yourself some credit. I mean, seriously. I know you have always been the strong one for your mom and your family, but cut yourself some slack here." After a few moments of silence, Maggie sniffed, wiping her face and nodding as she accepted her best friend's assessment.

Finally, Morgan prompted her, "Come on… get dressed. Let's go downstairs and have a real slumber party." Morgan suddenly remembered John's concoction in the kitchen and excitedly told her friend, "You won't believe the amazing pasta John whipped up!" Morgan's enthusiasm seemed to burrow its way into Maggie as she dressed; by the time they were ready to leave the suite, her friend even appeared excited about meeting everyone.

At the moment of their arrival in the kitchen, however, John and Patrick emerged from the office. For a breathless second, Morgan was unsure of the outcome of their conversation. However, she sighed heavily as the brothers grinned amicably at each other; she didn't see any blood or bruises on either man. When John saw her, his eyes lit up as he swiftly crossed the kitchen to wrap his arms around her.

"You are more beautiful than I remembered, my love," he told her, pulling her into his hard body for a kiss. As their mouths met, they both became breathless, everyone else in the kitchen ceasing to exist. When they finally had their fill for the moment, they pulled away from each other, noticing that there were more occupants in the room than before…and noticing that those occupants were all staring at them.

Well, perhaps not *everyone* was staring, Morgan thought. Jasmine was enveloped in Patrick's arms, and the couple were the only two that were not blushing…they were lost in each other. John broke the awkward silence by announcing, "Who's ready to eat? My masterpiece is ready now." Descending upon the stove, he began stirring the contents of the two pots, ensuring the quality of his creation.

Looking around, John seemed to notice Shannon for the first time, and he exclaimed, "Shannon, my old friend, how nice it is to see you! I didn't know you were arriving with my brother." The two men hugged, smiling companionably at each other.

The moment ended abruptly when Shannon unexpectedly slugged John in the shoulder, yelling, "That's what you get for Siobhan, mate!" The exchange startled Morgan, but as she moved to intervene, she was stopped by John's response.

"I know, you silly bloke...I deserve that. But I was right about the scrubber. And where is she now?"

Shannon looked around the kitchen until his eyes landed on Maggie. Sighing, he admitted, "The slag left me and ran off with some dickey dazzler rocker from London."

The silence that fell was thick and suffocating...until it was suddenly broken by Patrick chiming in, "Shut ye're gob, ye gingernut! Ye've known that lady muck was shaggin' those other blokes fer centuries." The sharp but jovial banter continued, all three of the men chiming in. Morgan noticed that their Irish accents became much thicker as they talked back and forth.

"My arse!" Shannon exclaimed, clutching his chest and feigning pain. "It's still a right solid kick in the bollocks."

As John scooped pasta from the pot into a large bowl, he shot back, "What are ya blatherin' on about, ya cacker, that brasser lass was playin' you from the start, and if ye're sayin' yer denyin' it, then your head's up your arse."

Patrick was laughing so hard that a tear had sprung up on his cheek. John looked years younger with the overlarge smile plastered to his face. Shannon's face was red for a moment, and Morgan feared that he was getting angry, but then he burst out laughing as he shouted, "Quit givin' me cheek, you louts! Especially in front of the lovely ladies!" Again, his gaze alighted on Maggie, causing her to blush.

"Cheek my arse, you apes," Shannon continued to jape. "Stop bitin' the back of me bollocks and step out of the way so I can get some grub. And lay off, I'm ready ter get locked, but not on an empty stomach." John quickly moved to the side, and Shannon scooped a mountainous heap of pasta and marinara onto his plate. Grabbing his beer, he walked to the table situated to the side of the kitchen, while Patrick prepared a plate for Jasmine.

"This looks delicious, John!" Jasmine exclaimed excitedly. "You've really outdone yourself."

Prying his eyes from Morgan's face, he nodded to Jasmine, acknowledging, "Yes, I remembered it was your favorite. I wanted you to have a warm welcome home, as well as create my masterpiece for my love." As he spoke these last words, his eyes locked with Morgan's, and she began to blush. Unresisting, she kissed his lips, touched deeply by his endearments.

Shannon cleared his throat loudly and grunted, "Come off it, ya hoor's melt, no more snogging in the kitchen. Yer makin' me narky with it." Morgan and Maggie both had to laugh at his grousing, and after Patrick and Jasmine had served themselves, Maggie piled some of the aromatic fare onto a plate for herself. Bringing the wine with her, she sat at the table across from Shannon.

As John approached, ready to prepare plates for Morgan and himself, he suddenly looked around and asked, "Where is Ma?" As if on cue, she entered the kitchen, Morgan noting that she looked refreshed and appeared quite a bit younger in her relaxed state. Smelling her Irish Moss soap, Morgan deduced that she must have just showered.

"Ma, you're just in time. How hungry are you tonight?" John called to her.

His mother checked the clock on the microwave and exclaimed, "John, its quarter past two in the morning…are we really sitting down to a meal at this time?"

John sighed audibly, obviously exasperated by his mother's practical musings, and then griped, "Ma, you all just returned home and everyone is famished. Besides, you've always loved my specialty. Here…" He handed her a plate, already prepared. "Why don't you join Patrick and Jasmine at the table. You'll feel much better after you eat."

Brunne complied, leaving John to feed himself and Morgan. The friendly chatter resumed at the table, with Patrick teasing Shannon mercilessly, Shannon sucking down his beer. When John and Morgan joined them, Shannon- nearly finished- stood and asked Maggie, "Can I get ye some more wine, me mot?"

Maggie swallowed audibly, handing him her glass and nodding. Morgan studied her for a moment, noticing that Maggie was being unusually quiet. Silently considering their earlier conversation, she could easily understand her friend's nervousness, as well as her anxiety regarding her premature feelings for Shannon. After pondering a bit longer, Morgan decided that she was glad her best friend was drinking wine tonight, as it would likely help loosen her up.

Upon returning to the table, Shannon handed Mag a full glass of wine. She took a conspicuously large gulp before setting her glass down on the table. Morgan took a long sip of her own wine, pleasantly surprised when John took the empty glass from her and stood to refill it.

A silence descended over the table while everyone ate, all focus concentrated on the consumption of the delicious meal. When finally, most plates stood empty, the table's occupants sated, Morgan suddenly restarted the conversation, exclaiming, "Oh, let me introduce you. I'd forgotten earlier that you hadn't all met." She started by nodding her head in Mag's direction, informing the group, "This is my very good friend, Maggie."

When Jasmine seemed puzzled by her presence, Maggie explained, "My power's out from the ice storm, so Morgan…that is, John said I could stay here for tonight."

A look of understanding crossed Jasmine's visage, and she spurted, "Oh my! That's why you two were in the room together! I sent Shannon to the guest suite, and John must have sent Maggie in before we arrived home."

As Jasmine distractedly puzzled this out before the other guests, Maggie's face bloomed to a red that nearly matched her hair; Shannon, despite his earlier rambunctiousness, looked as though he was struck for words. The two stared at each other momentarily…before pointedly deciding to stare at anything else.

Jasmine, finally realizing what she had been saying, gasped and hurriedly covered her mouth. "I'm so sorry. How embarrassing for you two. I was thinking out loud. Please forgive me." Patrick looked at her with a small grin, gulping his beer. As he set the empty glass down, Jasmine jumped up and grabbed it, speaking so fast it was difficult to understand her. "I'll gitchusumore, Patrick."

Patrick was right behind her with their plates; after setting the dishes on the counter, he and Jasmine left the kitchen together as John rejoined them at the table. Morgan looked at him, blinking innocently, and asked, "Did you forget something, dear?"

Remembering her wine, John retrieved it from the counter and handed it over. Smiling, he said, "It's my pleasure to serve you, my love."

This had Shannon guffawing loudly, and Maggie couldn't resist laughing out loud with him… which again had them both giggling in unison. Their laughter was contagious; even Brunne, dour throughout much of the meal, reluctantly chuckled along. It sounded surprisingly like a donkey braying, destroying all sense of composure at the table as John and Morgan burst into hilarity.

Hearing the laughter, Jasmine and Patrick soon returned to see what the ruckus was all about. Within moments, the laughter had snared them as well, and they couldn't help but join the fray. Soon, the kitchen and adjoining breakfast nook were alight with laughter, exacerbating more laughter, the occupants helpless and unable to stop. After what seemed like a long while, the group collectively paused for breath, allowing their stomachs and facial muscles some much needed relaxation.

Once they had all calmed, taking large sips from their drinks, the room fell silent. Then John announced, "I have chosen rooms for our guests. Please let me know if the arrangements are satisfactory."

Jasmine visibly tensed. Morgan suspected that she was irritated at being told where to sleep in her own home. John didn't seem to notice however, and continued.

"Mother," he started, turning to look at her. "Because the sidewalks are treacherously icy, I would like for you to sleep in the big house…at least for tonight. The bed in the library should offer the comfort you like, if that is satisfactory for you." Brunne did not argue for once, and was instead grateful that she could get settled in sooner rather than later. She also didn't mind not having to venture outside into the bitter cold.

Seeing that his mother was content with the arrangements, John looked to Jasmine and Patrick, beginning his explanation with, "You two have yearned to be together for so long, and I imagine some privacy would be much appreciated. If it would please you, I thought ma's quarters in back would be fitting." Jasmine sighed audibly and told her husband, "Thank you, John, it is very…thoughtful of you."

John nodded, continuing around the table. "Maggie, you already have your arrangement, and Shannon, you can take my office. The couch in there is quite comfy." At this announcement, the two redheads eyed each other briefly, and Morgan wondered if they were satisfied with their assignments.

Lastly, John turned to her, his lover, and lowered his voice. He then practically whispered to her, "You, my love, will come to bed with me." He brought Morgan's hand to his mouth and brushed kisses across her knuckles, causing butterflies to take flight in her stomach. She couldn't hold back the grin that widened on her face, or the blush that crept up her neck.

Shannon was apparently fed up with their PDA; standing abruptly, he stood up, pushing his chair back as he moved. Having consumed more libations than he had perhaps realized, he was a bit unsteady on his feet, his chair toppling over behind him, landing with a solid *thunk*. Looking down in confusion, his clumsiness became even more pronounced as his legs tangled with the chair's causing him to trip and fall with a resounding thud and an "Oaf!"

After a hearty laugh at Shannon's expense, Patrick and John went to help him to his feet, righting the chair and placing him carefully on its seat. "Me mate needs some *uisce*," Patrick murmured quietly, as if to himself.

"Aye; that he does," Brunne agreed.

Noting the puzzled looks from the younger ladies, Patrick clarified while walking to the kitchen. "Water. He needs some water."

Upon returning, Patrick placed the cool glass in front of his friend's face where it lay on the table before reaching for Jasmine's hand and prompting her to stand. Moving to his mother, he kissed her on the forehead and smiled. "Good night, Ma." She hugged him about the neck while Jasmine said her goodnights to the group, the two departing hand in hand.

As they turned the corner to the hall leading to the backyard, Patrick's hand cupped Jasmine's bottom; in response, Jasmine captured his hand, bringing his finger to her mouth and suckling it. Glancing toward Maggie, Morgan knew that her friend had also seen the interplay between the two lovers. Mag's expression seemed slightly embarrassed.

Obviously wishing to keep herself busy to avoid further uneasiness, Maggie stood and moved toward the mess in the kitchen. Like Morgan, she could quickly see that John, like most men, was quite the untidy cook, and she announced, "I will put away our dinner, but where is a bowl large enough for all of the leftovers, John?"

John began to argue, but Mag cut him off, walking toward the remnants of the sumptuous meal and saying, "I want to do it. I have a lot of nervous energy and I couldn't sleep if I tried." Hesitating a moment, she asked, "But where is your closest bathroom, first?" John pointed her in its direction, and she hastily took her leave of the lovers, the elder Kennedy, and the now-snoring Shannon.

Seeing that the remnants of the food were taken care of, Brunne excused herself, saying, "Goodnight, my son, and thank you for the delicious meal. And it was lovely to meet you, dear." She smiled to Morgan and then kissed them both on the forehead before leaving the kitchen.

As the door shut, the latch clicking, John reached over and grabbed Morgan, pulling her onto his lap. "I finally have you all to myself, my little vixen," he told her, looking lovingly into her eyes. As she gazed up at him, his hand found its way between her legs and swirled intimate circles, making her breath leave her in gasps, her hips bucking as she moaned into his mouth.

"You are so hot for me," he complimented her quietly, entering her with his two dominant fingers while taking over her mouth with his. She was like rubber in his arms, so pliant to his touches and the way he moved her on his lap. Beginning to lose herself, she suddenly remembered Shannon, head resting on the table before them; additionally, Maggie would be returning soon. Morgan pushed against the hand that had entered her slightly, reminding John that they were not alone.

His lips quirked up slightly as he moved his hand to her bottom, pulling her against the erection that strained the material between his legs and somberly expressed, "Morgan, I love you so much it scares me sometimes." He stared into her eyes as he made this admission.

Taking in his words, she studied him, sensing his vulnerability. She pulled him to her breast, tenderly whispering, "John, you could not ever love me too much. I…promise…you…" She emphasized these last three words by kissing him on his nose and cheeks. "I have without question fallen in love with you and I am yours."

Baring her heart to the man she loved, she studied him while he in turn studied her. They had both laid their vulnerabilities out for the other, and they felt naked and exposed for it. They each awaited judgment or condemnation…which did not come. Each had become previously accustomed to settling for less than what he or she wanted and needed; each found it difficult to fathom the complete and unyielding love the other offered.

Finally John said to her, "It is time that I take you upstairs, my love." With that, he gathered her up in his arms, carrying her upstairs where he did delicious things to her.

Chapter Thirteen

When Patrick and Jasmine arrived in the guest house, he immediately pulled her to him, her back to his chest, and kissed her neck. She could feel his hardened phallus pressing against her bottom, and she reached behind her to stroke him through his pants. Whispering in her ear as he fondled her with his finger, he uttered, "My beloved, I have waited too long to taste this."

"Mmmmm, Patch…I've waited too long to feel you," she admitted, turning around and facing him, causing his fingers to dislodge from where they intimately caressed her. Before she could bring her mouth to his, he raised his hand, suckling her essence from his fingertips as she watched him. Finally tasting her appeared to amp up his need to have her, and with a moan of desire he pulled her to him. Sharing a sultry kiss, they found their way to the bedroom together.

He laid her on the bed, her hair splayed out like a golden halo around her head. As he looked down at her, she watched him through half-lidded eyes, already wet in anticipation of the things they would do together.

Continuing to study her, he started the slow and seductive process of removing his shirt. His fingers nimbly released each button, drawing out the spectacle, not bothering in the slightest to hurry.

Impatient to have him, Jasmine decided that two could play at this game; hiking up her long skirt, she began fondling herself, bare beneath the flowy garment. Patrick's breath hissed out, his task suddenly becoming more hurried. She was delighted with her control over him, and she accentuated it by prodding herself over-dramatically while bucking against her own hand, sighing with pleasure. Her eyes closed to soak up the sensations, she didn't see that he had fully undressed…but she could feel his skin on hers when he blanketed her body with his.

"That was a dirty move, *leannan*," he told her. She could hear the smile in his voice. It did not take long for his hands to find their way up her shirt, pushing her bra up and circling caresses on her nipples, causing her to buck against him.

Sharing his amusement, she retorted, "But it got me what I wanted…you are naked and touching me deliciously."

Patrick could no longer contain himself. Suddenly pulling his hands apart, he ripped her blouse, exposing her full breasts. He began feasting on one budding nipple while dipping his fingers into her hungry mouth. She suckled him as though his digits contained life-affirming sustenance, she a starving person. Withdrawing his extremity from the hot moisture of her mouth, he brought his fingers down to fondle her other areola; he did not want to neglect it for long.

Unable to hold still under his ministrations, Jasmine began riding his thigh, leaving a sultry dampness in her wake. She wrapped her arms around his broad shoulders, holding him to her; however, she soon raised her hands to his head, pushing gently, attempting to relocate him to continue his delicious massage where she was wet for him.

Grasping her intent, he rose from her breasts, stopping his important task. Looking down at her, he used his free hand to pick up where his mouth had left off. With a smile that could be called evil in a different setting, he looked down at her and announced in a hoarse voice, "I dunt think so, me lack."

Jasmine's heart pounded against her breastbone. Only when he was in her sexual thrall did his Irish become so thick and sloppy, and thus far, she had only previously witnessed this transformation twice. Instantly, she understood that she was in for a very long night of very intense lovemaking, and she resigned herself to giving control of their activities to him. Almost always, she led their sessions while he gladly followed, giving her whatever she demanded… whatever she wanted or needed. But when he was in his present state, his sexual desires were nearly commands, and she loved to please him, giving him what he asked of her.

Seeing that she was pliant to his wishes, he claimed her mouth with his, sucking her lips between his roughly, pinching her breasts lightly before circling the nubs vigorously. When the breath she had been holding escaped in a rush, he snaked his tongue into her mouth, suckling her hungrily as she had suckled his fingers earlier. His shaft pushed painfully against his trousers, and he quickly removed the offending fabric, relieving the pressure.

Entering her with a force that pushed her into the mattress, he began to thrust into her with a punishing pace. She was so wet for him, and he was so worked up; very quickly they both climaxed, reverberations clamoring through them both. Patrick rested on top of her, bracing his weight on his elbows and his knees while remaining lodged within her.

After a few brief moments of respite, he withdrew from her. Descending her body, he stopped when his face was even with her nether region. He gazed up at her, watching her face, seeing her obvious excitement. Looking back down, seeing what her sprinkling of hair covered, he licked his lips as though preparing himself for a hearty banquet. Suddenly, he grasped the undersides of her thighs, thrusting them upward toward her head; in this position, he would be able to take her fully with his mouth while still sitting up.

Nearly upside down, Jasmine felt disoriented as he began to feast on her. He went about his business enthusiastically, soaking his face completely with her juices very quickly. She grasped the sheets to anchor herself, overwhelmed with the pleasure he was meting out. When the first orgasm ripped through her, she bucked, her legs thrashing involuntarily, needing a solid object to penetrate her core.

When she finally managed to see, blinking away the tears of pleasure that coursed down her face, she saw that his eyes remained wild…he was intent on continuing his meal. Stabbing his tongue deep within her, suckling, he drew yet more of her essence…the one that was unique to her; the essence of Jasmine. She orgasmed again and again into his mouth, but he could not be sated. Desperately needing a greater, more robust connection to him, she relinquished her death grip on the sheets, finding that she had to flex her fingers several times to relieve the cramps that had developed.

Reaching for him, she could just barely grasp his tip, and she played with it, twirling her finger in circles, feeling the wetness that had formed there. She knew that she had scored when he scooted his hips closer to her, bringing himself within range, leaving her able to circle her fingers around his shaft and stroke him to the base. With the first full stoke, she covered its entire surface with lubricant…the lubricant he had exuded throughout his fevered tasting of her. After several cycles, his grip of her hips began to loosen, his mouth not quite as tightly melded to her.

As he began pistoning forward, matching her gliding movements, he allowed her to sink slowly to the bed. He then entered her slowly, filling the void she had been feeling for an eternity while he lapped at her. Before long, his pace quickened, seeming to remember how badly he needed what she had to offer.

She felt a slight sting where he moved within her, most certainly caused by her recent vigorous activities. Pleasurable at first, it soon turned painful, and grimacing, she pulled back slightly.

Under normal circumstances, Patrick would stop immediately upon seeing her discomfort. However, in his sexual thrall, it seemed to spur him further, his strokes becoming harder and faster. Looking up, Jasmine could see that he would not respond to her non-verbal cue, refusing to slow down or adjust himself. Pulling back harder, she moved slightly away from him.

Jasmine laid her hands firmly on his chest, indignant at the vacant stare she was receiving from him. As he continued to pound into her, she increased the pressure on his chest, expecting him to stop. However, his expression remained one of intent concentration, and she began to feel frightened.

Looking at his eyes, it was as though he wasn't even there.

"Patrick," she said, feeling more and more alarmed. Finally, he seemed to snap to attention, his trance fading as he focused on her for the first time in a long while. Jasmine wasn't sure if it was her voice or her fearful expression, but as something at last penetrated his single-minded determination, his violent movements stopped. Becoming flaccid, he withdrew from her and studied her face for a moment.

"What is it, *a ghra mo chroi?*" he asked as he caressed her face.

She brushed his hand from her cheek, moving away from him on the bed. Standing, she grabbed the sheet, wrapping it around her torso before tucking it under her shoulders. Storming into the bathroom, she slammed the door behind her, snapping the lock in place for good measure. Against the quiet backdrop of the bedroom, it sounded as loud as a gunshot.

Lying alone in the bed, Patrick analyzed the interactions that had just taken place with Jasmine, working to discern the cause of her outburst. He had made love to her; if he was correct in his recollections, they had both orgasmed. Reaching between his legs, he touched himself gingerly, surprised at the rawness he felt there. Not in the shaft itself, but in the skin that covered o'er it. Fondling himself, he experienced a flashback of Jasmine- his *anam cara*- seeing her face as he moved inside her.

Instantly, his heart began pounding harder within his chest. Shifting images- Jasmine looking frightened- came to the forefront of his mine. Jumping up, he hurried to the bathroom door...the refuge to which she had escaped, locking herself in.

He spoke softly to her through the door. "*Ah gra*," he started, then translated for her. "My love, please open up. Please!" The last came out as a plea. While he couldn't recall all that had just transpired between them, he had a sinking suspicion that he had violated her horribly. His mind drifted, thinking about the first woman with whom he had ever had sexual relations, remembering a similar experience many years ago.

Having spent the night with her following that first sexual encounter, he had awakened her with his mouth. She had been quite delighted, and as he recalled this had led to multiple orgasms for them both. However, his memory stopped there; whatever proceeded from those last excruciatingly pleasurable orgasms was a complete blank. Later, he had been informed by the authorities that his actions towards the woman had been violent...akin to rape. If not for his prominent upbringing he likely would have spent some time incarcerated for his behavior. As it was, his family had been forced to make reparations for his actions, and his mother was unable to look him in the face for weeks.

For the life of him, he couldn't tease forward the memory of what had actually taken place; his mind was mute on the subject. It was not unlike that time at Shannon's pub, happily drinking ale…only later regaining consciousness in his bed…with a bandaged hand and a broken arm.

Interrupting his reverie, Jasmine abruptly burst from the bathroom door, marching past him. Grabbing her firmly by the arm, he swung her around to face him, his heart breaking at what he saw: fear, exuding from her as she looked at where he was grasping her arm. He let go of her immediately, recoiling as though he had touched a hot stove. As she quickly moved away from him, he clearly saw the hurt in her eyes, and the sheen of tears.

"Please, Jasmine," he pleaded with her, standing in front of the door that led out of the bedroom, blocking her exit. "Please, *céadsearc*, tell me what I have done. I do nut know." At hearing these words, she turned around to face him, searching his eyes. Weighing his words, it seemed, judging whether he spoke the truth.

Finally, she let out the big breath she had been holding, sitting down roughly in a corner chair. He began to speak again, but she stopped him with a raised hand. "I believe you, Patrick…although I don't know that I should. But something tells me that you really don't know what you were doing. It was like it…it wasn't you there…that was with me." She sighed deeply, seeming to gather herself, gesturing for him to sit on the bed across from her.

Waiting until he was seated, she took another deep breath and continued. "First, let me tell you something I have never told you before. I've not shared this with anyone ever, actually. It brings back memories too painful to think on much." He leaned forward and placed his hand on her knee, wanting deeply to comfort her; however, at his touch, she shooed him away. "I need a little space as I tell this, Patch." She shuddered slightly, considering her next words.

"I' twas when I was still young…but not too young. When I was first coming into my 'young lady' years. This was shortly after my eighteenth birthday. I wonder if he waited until then so as not to feel guilty about what he was doing," she mused, almost as though to herself.

"I felt like I was pretty safe in my home, since we had so many servants who looked after me when my ma was not around. And I did not think of myself as anything so desirable as would be used against my will…at least not like some of the other stories I had heard of that happened to other girls." Jasmine's accent thickened somewhat as she recounted her story, though normally it was almost undetectable.

Searching his eyes, she continued, "You see, in Romania, many girls from poorer families were sold at times of heightened poverty into slavery…and especially sex slavery. It wasn't that I didn't care that it was happening to some…I guess in my innocence I just didn't fully understand what it was that the news stories talked of."

Patrick watched her silently, developing a sick feeling in his gut. Jasmine, obviously seeing his concern and wanting to quash his sympathy, hurried to explain. "It was nothing like that. I was not ever sold. Well…at least not like that." Jasmine looked down, her shame evident as she remembered that time from her past. Patrick tentatively reached across to lift her chin, longing to look into her face. He did so gently, not wanting to startle her after their earlier encounter.

As Jasmine brought her eyes up to meet his, he told her emphatically, "Listen to me, *ma céadsearc.*" He entreated her with the intensity of his stare as he translated the Gaelic words for her. "'My beloved', Jasmine. You *are* my beloved. There is nothing you could ever tell me that would make me ashamed of you, and nothing that your bastard pa did to you that would ever make me think it was your fault what happened to yeh. I love you, my angel, and I donut want ye to be ashamed of somat happened to yeh when yeh was much younger."

Jasmine appeared to absorb his words, briefly looking fearful as he spoke with an accent that had become quite sloppy. Apparently deciding that he was not losing control again, she shook her head tersely and continued.

"Thank you, my love. Deep down, I know i' twas not my fault, but the hurt still remains." She took a deep breath, seeking courage to continue her story. "We were privileged, I think, and we would often have some of the traders stay in our home." After a pause, she said, "Many of them were prominent." He saw her throat move as she swallowed.

"Well, you've heard of where women marry, and in a way it's like they're property?"

She paused, awaiting his response. Quietly, he nodded and answered, "Aye."

"Then you've no doubt heard of where a woman or young lady has her honor taken from her, or in some cases she soils herself with her dalliances with young men; and then, whether it be of consenting relations that she had or not, her honor is ruined and she is no longer of any use to her family and is unlikely ever to marry, and in some cases is stoned to death."

"Aye, medieval customs to be sure, but I 'ave heard that it still goes on in some parts," he agreed with her.

She nodded, then explained, "My father sold my 'honor' to the highest bidder." She made air quotes as she spoke the word "honor", a wry twist to her mouth. She swallowed hard, obviously finding it difficult to keep her emotions at bay. As Patrick studied her face, beginning to understand the ghastly act of which she spoke, feelings of deep rage arose within him. His anger must have been clear in his expression, as Jasmine shrank back, making herself smaller in the chair. Seeing further evidence of the fear spawned by their earlier session in bed, Patrick took a deep breath.

Standing, he towered over her briefly, leaning down and gently picking her up, cradling her into his lap. When she began sobbing, he took her place in the rocking chair, whispering soothing words to her while he brushed her hair away from her face. His compassion, along with his gentleness, coaxed the tears from her, and soon her body was racked with deep, trembling sobs. Despite earlier occurrences, Patrick could still feel the great trust she placed in him as she snuggled into his neck, her tears running down his chest. He patiently rocked her and stroked her, paying soft kisses to her forehead.

Her pain spent, she sat up and looked at him, quietly stated, "This one man…Master Dolph…as I was forced to call him…was the highest bidder." She looked away from him for the moment, apparently too ashamed to look him in the eye, and he gave her the space. Resting his chin on the top of her head and holding her to him, he avoided looking at her face.

After what seemed like an eternity, she went on. Patrick thought it likely that she wanted to finish recounting those awful events as quickly as possible rather than drag it out. "He was very kind to me at first, and actually waited patiently for a while. My father had sold me to him for the summer, although I was told that he was a distant uncle taking me to his home for holiday." Patrick tightened his arms around her slightly, his hands caressing her skin.

"The first time, he made it seem like a game that he had only just begun playing with me. It was after I had been there for several days. This, I believe, was his vacation home, and he did not regularly employ servants there, so I was all alone with him. It was a country estate. I couldn't have run had I tried. Not that I would have at first." Silent tears began to fall and she said haltingly, "I was so stupid…so silly and naïve. He made me feel…special."

Patrick smoothed her hair back, hugging her until this difficult moment passed, kissing her shoulder. When she had been quiet for a long time,

Patrick squeezed her and prompted, "I am still listenin', my lil' darling."

"So the game..." She relaxed into him, describing her abuser's manipulations. "It started out with him sayin' he cared for me a great deal, and because that was so, he would let me be like a big girl and share some of his spirits with dinner. This went on for the first several nights...only, each time he would say I could only stay up late or drink with him if I would do this or that...It usually entailed me taking off some of my clothing at the table. But he wanted me to follow his special instructions. Like he would want me to be seated already without a shirt when he came in."

She stopped for a moment, breathing deeply. Finally, she said, "After about the fifth day, he plied me with alcohol and instructed me to sit in his chair with nothing on. Usually he would take some time in getting to the dining room so that I had nearly finished my meal before he entered...but not that day. That day he was in there when I got there. I was confused and embarrassed because it was one thing to sit half-dressed behind the cover of a table while he walked in, and something completely different to walk into a room without a stitch, with instructions to sit where he had seated himself at that." Patrick's muscles tensed again as she recounted these events, but this time Jasmine seemed to find a sense of security in his anger.

"I hesitated, of course, and he smiled at me, and then pushed himself away from the table. He was nude from the waist down and he was…erect, although I didn't understand the mechanics of sex at the time. I still thought babies were born through the belly button and came out of kissing." She shivered for a moment, but then persevered. "I was so confused and scared. When I started to turn around, he grabbed my wrist and pulled me to him…he…put my hand on him down there, and made me touch him."

Patrick forced himself to take deep breaths as he held her. When Jasmine, struggling to breathe, asked him to loosen his hold on her, he noticed how tight his embrace had become and forced himself to relax.

"He explained it to me while he did this, like he was my teacher and he was educating me. It was like he thought he was doing me a favor…teaching me about how to touch a man. After he finished, he made me drink more. Well, that's an understatement," she admitted. "Truthfully, he held it to my lips, and I was in so much shock that I swallowed it. By the time he carried me to his bed, I was good and drunk and had completely forgotten about my nudity. I considered the situation passively…almost as if from an outsider's point of view.

"That is, until he put his mouth on me down below." She gripped his arm, seeking to distract him from looking at the place on her body that had been so forcefully used against her will. Patrick could not keep his hands from shaking, and he kept them clenched together, knuckles white, where they met around her waist.

She closed her eyes to finish her story, as if shutting out her current surroundings to bring these past horrors to the forefront. "He...did things with his mouth...things that...felt good...to my body." As she made this confession, she curled up tightly in his arms, making herself very small as she seemed to await his rejection and condemnation.

Sensing that she was conflicted, Patrick prompted, "He made ye orgasm then?" Her breath hissing out gave him the answer to his question. Standing up and holding her in his arms, he carried her gently across the room and into the bedroom, laying her back on the bed. Her hair fell around her as it had earlier. Looking down at her, the contrast from earlier was...astonishing. She still looked an angel, but this time her beauty seemed tragic.

Patrick planned to remedy it. Lying on his side next to her, he pulled her toward him and took her face in his hands. "Listen to me, my little lover. A body can't help what it does when things are being done to it...especially not against its will, and not when spirits are involved. You can nay let this get your goat. I tell ya, this man had his way with you in a very conniving way. He groomed ya so as to try ter confuse ya an' make ya not know his scoundrellin' ways."

When she opened her mouth to argue, Patrick shook his head. "You canna argue with me about this, love. The sameat happened to one of my young cousins, only this really was her uncle. It was when I was a wee lad, but I still member the story, though I canna tell ya what happened ta the man that did it. He was nay seen after me kinfolk got holt of him."

As Jasmine glanced tentatively up at him, she evidently found comfort in his expression, kind and open. An awkward smile broke out on her face. Bringing her mouth to his, she kissed him squarely on the lips. That kiss communicated her intense gratitude far better than any words could have ever done. Returning the kiss, he soon felt it deepen as they embraced fully, wrapping arms and legs around each other. When their passion was spent, he folded her in his arms and laid her head on his chest.

After lying still for a few moments, the lack of sleep for the previous thirty-six hours finally caught up with him. He distantly felt Jasmine grab the comforter from the foot of the bed, covering them both. Before sleep claimed him, he opened his eyes one last time. The look on his lover's face as she gazed quietly at him…could only be described as peaceful. Closing his eyes, contentment washing over him, he wrapped his arms about her, cradling her, and fell to sleep.

Chapter Fourteen

Jasmine woke at the crack of noon, smelling the aroma of her man, freshly showered. He stood next to the bed, sipping his coffee and staring down at her awakening figure, studying her. "Have I ever told ye that yer the most beautiful woman upon first waking that I have e'er laid eyes on?" he asked her, bringing a smile to her lips.

"You have, my lover…twice. Once at the castle estate, and the other time when we woke in that hotel in Chicago."

He smiled in his masculinely beautiful way, announcing, "Well then, I been doin' right by ya, lass."

Jasmine turned over, lying flat and exposing her nakedness to his appraising eye. He did not break his gaze from her as he set his coffee cup on the side table, sitting next to her on the edge of the bed. He was silent for a moment as if choosing his words carefully. First looking at him askance, she then reached for his hand. Grasping her hand in return, he pulled her up to a sitting position, facing him.

"I must tell ye about sumpthin' that I did when I was a might bit younger."

Feeling momentarily alarmed, she studied his face. Letting him know that he had her full attention, she told him, "You can tell me anything, Patrick." The look of regret that briefly crossed his face caused her fear to spike again, anxious about what he would reveal...especially after their time the night before.

When he began his confession, he looked away, appearing to study a dot on the floor. It was obvious that he could not bring himself to meet her eyes while he spoke. "I donut think I be a good enough man for ye, Jasmine."

She stopped breathing for a moment. He could *not* be leaving her...not now, when she had just gotten him back! And not after she had just trusted him with such deeply personal information! Her heart raced for a moment as she grabbed at his arm, turning him to look at her. "No, Patrick! You stop it. I won't have this. You gave me your unwavering word that you would not be ashamed of me no matter what, Patrick, and I'll be damned if I can't give you the same gift." She could hear the anger in her own voice as she grabbed his face, staring intently into his eyes.

Under her unwavering gaze, his emotional dam appeared to break open. As his tears began to silently fall, he dropped to his knees in front of her, burying his head in her lap. She gripped his hair, holding his head as he sobbed into her thighs. In an effort to soothe him, she stroked his back as he had done for her a few scant hours before.

After a short while, he lifted his head and looked at her. The tears remained on his face, there for her to see- as though they were proof of his guilt- and making heavy eye contact with her, he confessed his sins to her, the guilt straining his voice. He told her about what had transpired between him and his first lover, Breanna. He then spoke of the events that had occurred at his buddy's pub: two occurrences when he- similar to the previous night- had behaved despicably, and in a manner very unlike him. When he finished, he broke eye contact, his head hanging low…having already condemned himself.

Jasmine sat quietly for a while, considering the story he had just told her. The behavior done by the man he described- the man who had stared blankly and emptily at her the night before- was *not* her Patrick. He had appeared possessed…but not by an evil spirit; instead, her beloved seemed to be on auto-pilot. A wisp of thought floated through her mind, too ephemeral for her to catch, and she immediately decided that she needed to know more.

"Patrick, can you tell me a bit more about the first time it happened with the girl? Breanna?" She implored him to share, coaxing him from his personal courtroom of self-condemnation where he acted as his own judge, jury, and executioner.

Finally, he began to discuss it. "Well, it was a wee bit after I'd begun college, so it was...let's see... when I was nineteen years old." His eyes stared off at some far off point as if trying to recall those past events. "I had gotten leave from university to go home for the weekend, and it was the first time Breanna and I were to...er, consummate our relationship." He eyed her for a moment before admitting, "She was me first, that girl, and it promised to be a right exciting adventure to bed her for the first time. We had been seeing each other for more than a year by tha' time."

Looking shyly from the corner of his eye, he was evidently gauging her reaction as he discussed his previous affair. She carefully kept her face blank, and he continued. "So, I was beside myself the week before. Had tests ter study fer and all, so didna get much in the way of sleep for a while before that weekend, then had to take a train and a ferry and then another train to reach home before I made it finally to her."

Interrupting for a moment, Jasmine raised her hand slightly and asked, "So you hadn't slept in how long, exactly?"

He thought about her question for a few seconds, calculating before telling her, "I dunno that I could rightly answer yer question, lass. I'm not sure that I slept more than thirty minutes at all that week." He seemed taken aback by his own answer.

Her next question appeared to surprise him as well. "And when you had the row in the pub, what had been going on before that happened?"

He stared into space again, trying to recall the events that had preceded the brawl. Finally, he told her his conclusion. "That must ha' been…yes, that was about a week past me da's wake. I know it because when I was laid up in bed was when me great auntie Gertrude finally managed to make it to the estate. She groused at me for her having to walk so many stairs, what with me da having jus' been laid to rest and all."

Jasmine was beginning to come to her own conclusions about his state of mind during these seeming absences. "When we were together in Indianapolis in the hotel room…" She paused to give him a second, making sure that she had his attention before asking, "You had been awake a while awaiting my arrival, had you not?"

A small smile on his face, he gave a small nod, agreeing, "Could nay sleep until ye arrived safely in my arms."

"And who drove you from New York after you and Shannon arrived?" she continued.

His smile widened as he told her, "'Tis Shannon's first time in the states. I canna make a man tha's not ever been here do tha drivin'. 'Twould be reckless."

Feeling her face reddening slightly with exasperation, she demanded, "And you didn't think it was reckless of you to stay awake for days, Patrick Shea Kennedy?!" His laugh finally breaking forcefully through his smile, he wrapped his arms around her waist, kissing her lips. Though returning the kiss with a throaty sigh, Jasmine knew that it would do nothing to improve the tongue lashing she was about to give him.

When he finally pulled away from her, sitting back on the floor, his smile remained in place, prompting her to glare and demand, "Just what is so bloody funny?" Breaking out in near-hysterical laughter, the tears began flowing down his cheeks again. Having had enough, she jumped up and stormed across the room, beginning to pace.

Finally recognizing her evident anger, he settled down to try and answer her question. "I just confessed to you that I raped a girl when I was younger, and last night I nearly raped you." He began to sober as he explained, finishing very seriously with, "And you are admonishing me for not getting enough sleep."

The vulnerable look Jasmine saw in his eyes made her heart go out to him, and she quickly went to him, sitting, and then taking his face in her hands. He made a weak attempt to pull away, but she held him firmly and seriously, looking him in the eye as she said, "Patrick, my love. I don't think you did the things you think you did. At least not of conscious mind." She waited, watching for his comprehension about her speculation; when he continued to look at her with eyes full of lost hope, she hurried to enlighten him.

"Patrick, I think you had what my mother used to call a 'brain fit'. I think the American word for it is 'seizure'." Hope flared briefly in his face… guarded hope, haunted by his past, but struggling to understand that those egregious sins he had carried for so long were not truly his transgressions.

Finally, he pulled away from her, stating, "Well, *ma shearc*, it is still so that I nearly raped you. How ye can ever look at me with love in ye're eyes and wanting in ye're heart is beyond me." Backing toward the room's door, his expression one of dejection, he said, "And besides, we canna know, now can we?"

His tone held a finality, telling Jasmine that Patrick had made up his mind that they were not to be together. She jumped to her feet and ran to stop him. Grabbing his arm, she pulled with every ounce of her strength, knowing that with her petite figure and his large stature she would have very little effect.

Jasmine fought to hold him, afraid that once he walked out the door, he was gone for good. But to no effect; he continued toward the door, dragging her behind him as though her weight was nothing. Desperately, she screamed, piercing the air and causing him to stop and cover his ears. Finally, he turned to look at her.

"Please, Patrick. Listen to me. Please!" she begged him, her tears gathering.

He looked down at her as he considered for a few moments, finally telling her, "I donut think I can, me love." The anguish was plain in his voice as well, and in tandem tears fell from both of their faces. Swallowing his despair, he wiped his cheeks before embracing her, holding her tightly for a moment.

Pushing her gently away, he looked plaintively at her and spoke, begging her to understand, his emotions more intense than anything she had ever experienced with him. "Donut ye see, Jasmine? How could we move past this? I have violated ye…violated the sacred boond…the trust that ye have in me. And after all that ye have been through…first with that Dolph character, and then that which your paps did ter ye and The Market business. I can nay forgive meself fer what I did ter ya, and I will nay be responsible for ye being tied to the likes of meself. Ye deserve a might bit better, ye do. I am no good enough fer ye."

Grabbing her arms in desperation, he shook her, pleading for her to understand. He sank to his knees before her, hugging her legs to himself as if they were his lifeline. Tears flowed freely again from both of them, and Jasmine sank to the ground with him, holding him as he held her, his desperate need to feel her palpable.

Time froze as they lay on the ground next to each other, wrapped up in each other's arms and legs, eyes staring into eyes. Finally, Jasmine broke the silence. In a hoarse voice that was nearly a croak from her tears, she told him, "If you leave me, Patrick, it would kill me. I could not take it. Not after waiting so long to have you. I couldn't survive losing you just like that."

He closed his eyes for a moment, blocking out the sight of her. When he opened his mouth to speak, Jasmine could see that he was not yet able to get past what he had done to her; quickly, she stopped him before the words could leave his lips.

"Listen to me, Patrick." Her voice was still hoarse, but getting stronger with each word, a command with which he must comply. Seeing that she had his attention, she continued. "My supposition of you having seizures is not just conjecture to excuse your behavior. I love you deeply, but even my affections hold some boundaries that would be tested by you purposefully and violently assaulting an innocent." He listened to her intently, but the look on his face showed that he was still skeptical.

"I have for some time held an interest in the medical arts," Jasmine explained. "Do you remember when the man from the village brought his young daughter to me who had the horrible rash?" Recognition lit his face for a moment, so she continued. "If you will remember, I did not stop until I found the herbs that helped the poor child, and her skin never looked better." A slight smile began to touch the corners of his mouth, but Jasmine could not tell if his smile was cynical or optimistic; probably the former.

Continuing her explanation tirelessly, she told him, "Since I have been in America, I have watched endless medical television shows." When he quirked an eyebrow, she explained, "What else was I to do when I had told John that I had a headache, but wanted to stay in my room so that I could seek respite from his dominance for a while?"

As she mentioned his brother, Patrick's countenance softened. He certainly knew how miserable it had been for his beloved to be with John, a man who she did not love, forced to maintain the façade in order to keep her love affair with Patrick secret. Jasmine had confided in him previously, expressing her pain in that dark time. Once, during sex with John, she had actually cried out Patrick's name as she climaxed; thankfully, John had been too drunk to hear or notice.

Finally, making her point, she concluded, "So, one of my favorite shows has discussed sleep disorders relating to lack of sleep being a cause of brain attacks, or seizures." She watched a variety of expressions chase across his face for a moment before telling him, "There is a test they can administer to check to see if you are having seizures when you… go stupid amounts of time with inadequate sleep." She said this last part accusingly, daring him to disagree with her. When a wide smile split his face, she knew that she had won him over; at least enough to have the tests performed.

Abruptly, Patrick stood, bending down to pull her into his arms. He picked her up, cradling her against his chest, and carried her through the bedroom into the bathroom. Setting her gingerly onto the granite counter top, he brought his face very close to hers and said, "*Ma shearc*, I donut know what I would do without ye looking after me, but I bloody sure don't want ter have ter find out."

With this, he captured her mouth, holding her very close. Jasmine wrapped her legs around his waist and pulled him to her as they made love with their tongues. Finally, he pulled back and looked down at her; smiling, he reached in the drawer, pulling out a bottle that she immediately recognized. *He must have put that bottle in the drawer while I slept.* She was excited to find out what he had planned for her.

Turning, he started the bath water, and soon the steam began to rise. Upending the contents of the small glass bottle over the tub, he poured out her personal mixture of dried lavender, witch hazel, and other soothing and healing herbs. When he was finished, he turned to face her. The desire she saw in his face caused her to become wet very quickly; had she been standing, she would have had trouble holding herself up, her knees weak from the strength of her own longing for him.

Not willing or able to wait for the tub to fill completely, Patrick sidled up to his beloved and pulled her face to his. Gently pushing her back, reclining her against the mirror, his hungry expression projected his need to taste her; licking his lips in anticipation, he buried his face between her thighs. This time, he was much gentler with her, his touch tentative as he noticed the reddened areas he had caused the night before. Jasmine would be seriously surprised if his own genitals weren't tender. If he was sore, he would probably not mention it, likely deciding that he deserved it. He continued to lap at her, obviously savoring the flavor that danced on his tongue, reveling in the moans that he elicited from her.

Within a few short minutes, she began moving her hips, riding his face. Patrick turned to look at the bathtub and, seeing that it was three-quarters full, picked her up, stepping into the water while carrying her. He seated himself, guiding her legs around him so that she straddled him. Reaching behind her slowly, she turned off the water. As Patrick watched her muscles ripple as she moved, her body rubbing against his, he began groaning passionately.

After staring down at him for a moment, Jasmine licked her lips and lifted herself, descending his body slowly, with a cat-like, sensuous crawl. As she moved, she roughly pushed his legs aside, smiling up at him while licking her lips. His cock jerked in anticipation, and she smiled triumphantly as she felt its movement on her chin.

Patrick understood her desire to take control during their lovemaking, and he appeared greatly satisfied as he allowed her to direct them. By now, he had learned that the things she did to him were unparalleled. No one could ever match the pleasure she gave him; should he have followed through with his mad plan to leave her, Jasmine was certain that his remaining years would be a life of celibacy.

As she took his scrotum into her mouth, his breath left him in a sudden rush. She commanded his full attention, taking him, knowing exactly what turned him on most. She suckled him, alternating between soft caresses and more pressured suction. Watching his face, she brought her hand up and fisted it around his shaft. She wanted to please him; do things to him with her mouth that could turn a priest into a sinner.

She continued her sensuous massage, capturing his entire consciousness. She moved her mouth from balls, ascending his shaft with her tongue, licking hot circles with increasing pressure until she reached the mushroom head. Turning her face to the side, she suckled him into her mouth, pressing his tip into the delicate skin of her cheek. Patrick suddenly gripped the side of the tub as he exploded, sending hot jets spewing into her throat. With wicked satisfaction, she swallowed and smiled at him, moving to lie in the tub next to him.

The soothing herbs relaxed their bodies. After some time, Patrick evidently needed to feel more of her; to taste her release, and to give back what she had so generously given him.

He looked down at her, studying her features. She closed her eyes, absorbing the sensations that enveloped her. He reached out and gently ran his thumb over her dark lashes adoringly. He caressed her silken blonde hair that he so often admired; it was darker during the winter months, but she grew it longer for him then, though she knew he loved it just the same. His fingers gently traced across her face, eating up what he so often described as her flawless beauty. She opened her eyes, looking up at him; his expression was one of deep longing, cherishing the softness of her skin, needing to feel it.

Gazing into his eyes, she tried to project to him all of the love and trust she felt. As he saw the depth of her feelings, he appeared overwhelmed and the emotions assailed him. He brought his mouth to hers, kissing her and holding back his awestruck tears.

Their kiss, chaste at first, deepened until she was breathing heavily into his mouth. Releasing her lips, he announced, "*Ma shearc*, I must taste you. My appetite burns to be satisfied by your flavor." As she watched his lips brush down her face, moving to her neck and then her collarbone, she moved against him, enticing him. However, he held his ground and continued to place kisses on her delicate areas. Lazing for a while at her right breast, he twisted the left nipple into a tight little peak before continuing his descent with a side trip that brought him to her hip bone.

When Jasmine was sure that she could take it no longer, he arrived at his destination, lifting her hips out of the water and bringing her to his mouth. He watched her face as his tongue caressed the first light stroke…where her nerve endings were already firing deliciously, causing her hips to lift from the water as she gave him better access to her. He held her there, dining on her luscious fruit and basking in the ambrosia she created for him.

As she let out soft moans, she could feel his passion intensify, his shaft beginning to lengthen and harden again, anxious to have her. He didn't appear ready to give it what it wanted just yet, however, and he continued his slow and sensuous kneading.

When the pleasure began to spike, he pulled back slightly, lightening his touch until her movements slowed. When she relaxed, he increased the pressure, bringing her to the edge of climax. Over and over he repeated this assault on her senses, causing her to alternate between panting and lying back quietly, soaking up the pleasure he provided.

When the wave of pressure increased to a nearly painful crest, he lifted his head and looked into her eyes. She knew that she must appear drunk, watching him through glazed eyes as he swiftly sheathed himself to the hilt, causing them both to cry out. Evidently he still was not ready for their erotic dance to end, as he pulled his shaft from her core, leaving only the tip poised at her entrance, holding her hips to keep her in the desired position.

The cauldron of her passion bubbling over, she opened her eyes wide and groaned, "Don't stop!" Hearing the pleasure in her voice, he smiled at her and continued to grip her hips. When she saw his intention to still hold back, she frantically began pulling on him, trying to impale herself, whimpering to him again. "Please Patch...I need you inside me." He studied her face for a moment, as if wanting to burn her expression into his memory to hold for all time; he then entered her with a force that caused water to slosh onto the floor. He drove into her over and over, relentless, until they both cried out. When the storm finally calmed, they settled into an embrace, breathing each other in.

Small shivers danced over Jasmine as their bath began to cool, causing ripples in the water. Patrick pulled her against him more securely and kissed her thoroughly on the lips, with a sigh, whispering, "*Ma fiorghra*, ye have turned cold. I must warm ya."

Enchanted, she smiled at him, as he picked her up and stepped out of the tub with her. Fetching a large fluffy towel, he carried her into the living room and placed her on the sofa, covering her with a quilt as he set to work building a fire.

Once the flames were roaring, he sat on the couch next to her, pulling her onto his lap. She snuggled against his chest, wrapping the blanket around him so that they were cocooned together, skin to skin, in a tranquilly warm bliss. Patrick breathed a sigh of deep satisfaction. Jasmine felt that they were one, united, and she knew that if they died that very minute, they would both be at their happiest moment.

Jasmine's chest swelled to bursting, so full of the love and happiness she felt only when she was with her beloved. She couldn't help but stare at him as he held her; she was afraid that, if she took her eyes off of him for too long, the present situation would come undone, and she would be back with her husband.

Chapter Fifteen

After sitting together, basking in each other's presence, Jasmine felt grateful that she could finally be with the one that she cherished…who cherished her in return. She was thankful she would no longer be forced to stay with John. He did not love her, and she had always felt compelled to be for him someone other than who she was.

Her thoughts of John heralded the memory of what she and her husband had done together immediately before she went to pick up Patrick. She was unable to stop a gasp from escaping her, and the color drained from her face.

Startled, Patrick shifted her on his lap, looking at her face. "What is it, my love?" he asked anxiously, alarmed at her sudden pallor.

She couldn't bring herself to look at him; she was so ashamed of what she had done. But how could she expect him to share his heartaches with her…if she did not trust him in the same way? Admittedly, however, it was not the same.

Jasmine found it difficult to pull air into her lungs, and she started to feel dizzy. She knew that she must look bad when Patrick pushed her head between her legs, telling her, "That's it, *ma shearc*, breathe."

He massaged the back of her neck while she bent over, calming to a degree.

Finally, he looked at her and said, "Ye've calmed down. Now...tell me what is wrong. After all that we have shared, you shouldna be scairt to tell me anything."

Jasmine wasn't so sure...especially considering what it was that she needed to tell him. Finally looking him in the eye, her tears welled. She knew that what she must disclose would destroy the trust that they had worked so hard together to build. Worse, she knew how much it would hurt Patrick to know that, even after her husband had agreed to let her go, she had been with John.

"Patrick, do you remember that day when I told you that John was letting me go, and that we could be together?" She searched his eyes as she began her confession, wanting to find...what, she didn't know.

When he nodded, she took a deep breath, stalling for a moment to decide how to hit him with the news of her infidelity. Steeling herself, she gathered her courage and admitted, "I was so excited after I called you, Patrick, and right away I packed the kids, and then myself. We were all ready to go, including your ma...and then I went to find John to tell him."

She spoke rapidly, wanting so much to get this unpleasant admission out of the way as quickly as possible. However, when the time arrived to discuss the gory details, she stopped, unable to make the words leave her mouth. She opened her mouth, then closed it, trying to decide how to tell him.

After several moments of silence, he prompted her, "Spit it out, love. The wonderin' is likely harder to take than the truth ye'll tell me."

You're wrong, she thought dejectedly. Finally, she said, "Patrick, I went to find John, and I did…I found him with Morgan. And there's something I hadn't told you about her…about how they got together."

Searching her eyes in silence, he patiently awaited her story. Finally, she said, "John and I were trying to come up with a way to make it work for ourselves. It had become so dreadful between the two of us, and we finally decided that it was time to end it, or do something different…so that we actually liked each other again, and could live together without the constant animosity."

Patrick listened, wrapped up in her story, and Jasmine knew that he understood the misery that had been caused by her marriage to John. Her eyes pleaded with him to understand, prompting him to massage her shoulder and tell her softly, "Go on."

"Well, I'm not sure that you know this about me, Patrick, but I sometimes have an attraction for other women." She paused, awaiting his condemnation. Cursing, she knew this would be the first in a long line of things about her that would disappoint him.

To her surprise, he grinned and told her, "I already knew that, love. It's you that doesna remember. The time in Chicago, at the pub we went to, there was a lil' miss that you was all over, that fancied you some as well…that is, until her husband showed up with 'is knickers in a twist."

Jasmine vaguely remembered the incident he described, and she felt a sense of relief for a few seconds. Smiling, she exclaimed, "You knew, and you were okay with it, Patrick?"

He caressed her cheek and said, "It was bloody fun, watchin' the two of ya, actually, and if ye be rememberin' correctly, beddin' ya that night was somethin' of an epic time."

She smiled briefly…at the memory, as well as at his thickening accent, thinking he must still be extremely tired to have such a lose tongue, as he normally spoke with less of the Irish accent she was currently hearing.

Snapping out of her reverie, she turned to face him again, explaining, "So, John and I, after a huge fight, and him furious with me, because we hadn't…

that is…" She searched for the right words, and Patrick, seeming to understand her difficulty, patted her on the thigh, comforting her.

Still tripping over her words, she managed to get out, "He couldn't touch me, because I didn't respond to him in the way he liked." As she made the admission, she closed her eyes, feeling the rejection from her husband as if it had just happened.

Patrick worked to comfort her, and Jasmine knew he had an acute understanding of unmet passion and unsated longing. "That, *ah gra*, is because ye werena made for him, and ye are nay right to be together. Ye were made fer me, *ma shearc*, and ye are perfect fer me, *cara*." He kissed her lips, making sure his statement sunk home. She let his lips roam hers, passively accepting his invasion as his tongue sank in, exploring. Finally, she gave a soft nudge to his chest. She wanted to get this out…if she didn't finish soon, she felt sure that she would explode.

"I have to tell you this, Patchy. You won't feel the same way about me once it's said." She felt so forlorn, Patrick looking saddened by her distress. However, he could obviously feel the apex of her story looming, and he was beginning to have difficulty breathing himself.

"Verra well, love. Tell me what it is that you ha' been tryin' ter tell me."

She swallowed hard, persisting with her dreaded monologue. "So, Morgan was our realtor when we bought this place, and I had always felt that he was attracted to her. It was in the way his face would light up when she would walk into the room, or the way his eyes followed her billboards anytime we passed them on the interstate.

"When we were in the market to buy, she was still married to her bastard husband, and I don't think she is the kind that cheats. But once his affair turned into something bigger, he left her, and then it was like a light switch turned on inside her. I mean, really! She had always been attractive, but suddenly, it was like overnight, her billboards started popping up everywhere, and they really showed off her assets. She was stunning."

Patrick gave a slight nod; not as much in agreement as in acknowledgment of what it was that she was conveying.

"So, after one of our really big fights...well, when I say fight, I mean one-sided monologue where he yells at me while pounding his fist, and I listen quietly, biding my time until he spends his rage and no longer frightens me." It was a statement of fact, not a plea for pity, and Patrick, understanding, didn't offer unwanted sympathies.

"When he finally calmed down, I was at a breaking point where I knew something had to change. It was just before Christmas, and I couldn't stomach the idea of spending the holiday in such miserable companionship. I knew that he was seething from sexual frustration, and that the only chance for us to change for the better was to somehow bring something to our bed that would allow him to spend some of his sexual energy.

"I had received an invitation to the yearly Christmas party that Morgan's boss throws for their customers, and it's what gave me the idea. It was really hard to bring it up to him. I thought he would be angry with me for even asking. But he was actually excited by the idea, and said that he would approach her at the party. When he finally had the chance to talk to her alone, she was in the kitchen with her boss, and John thought that they were…having an affair together.

"I think he was wrong. When he told me of his conclusion later, I recalled having seen her boss and his wife together, and for some reason felt that it was unlikely. There's just something about him that makes me think he wouldn't do that to his wife."

She paused a moment, feeling the dryness of her throat. "Would you like some wine, darling?" she asked him, restless and needing to move around as much as she needed to quench her thirst. He was silent as she rose, fetching the wine and pouring him a glass of her favorite red. Sitting back down next to him, she took a long swallow before continuing.

"Where was I? Yes…so we wanted to bring her in, but John thought that she might have been seeing her boss. When we came home that night, it was…horribly disappointing. John had stopped sleeping in my bed long before this, and I was terribly lonely. When we had left to go to the party, he had told me that if things went as planned, maybe he'd help me warm my bed that night."

Patrick gasped, but she waved his concern away, taking another sip of wine. "Before we pulled into the driveway, I was close to tears. It felt as though my hopes and dreams of ending my dreary existence had been dashed in one encounter. And John did not, in fact, sleep in my bed that night, though he was kinder to me after that. In fact, our interactions became cordial enough that I actually felt comfortable suggesting that he try to contact Morgan again."

Her expression darkened for a moment as she recalled, "It's quite peculiar, looking back. He only ever seemed to smile at me when I mentioned her name. All other times he wore his trademark scowl." She mused quietly for a moment before explaining, "So strange, it was…though I wanted nothing to do with John, and did not desire to be in a relationship with him, or to be intimate with him, it saddened me to know that the thought of another woman gave him pleasure, when I was so undesirable to him." She made this admission plainly and honestly.

"But I still encouraged him to make contact with her. For the longest time, he said he was considering it, until finally, one day he came to me with a plan." Directing her stare at Patrick's face, she wanted to stress the significance of what she was saying.

She explained to him that John had come up with an idea: they would not disclose to Morgan the significant issues that plagued their marriage. John would tell his prospective lover that he was unable to be intimate with his wife; that he could not become aroused by her, because Jasmine favored their children too much. It would be better, he had reasoned, because it would make Morgan sympathetic to Jasmine's "plight"…and in the event that Morgan agreed to join them, she would not be shocked by John's overwhelming need of sex.

"It was not far from the truth, he had told me, since he was in fact no longer aroused by me. In that, I suppose we were even, because I was not aroused by him." She finished her glass of wine as Patrick downed the last of his, and he rose to refill them.

When he returned, she finished, "So, with the plan set in place, he made contact with her." Jasmine stared into space for a moment, remembering that fateful day…which had actually not been that many days ago.

"What happened the first time between Morgan and me was amazing, Patrick. I wish I could lie to you and say that it was mediocre, but I cannot, and I wouldn't choose to. As much as I want you to be proud of me, I can no longer live that way."

Patrick looked puzzled by her statement; seeing his confusion, Jasmine explained, "I never quite felt I could be myself with John. I can't quite put my finger on it, but I never felt I was able to. Maybe it's that we're really not right for each other, and maybe it's my persistent lack of confidence. Whatever it is, I have never felt strong enough with him to be myself." She was silent for a moment, and then said, "It's no way to live, and I'm happy that I can be myself whenever I'm with you. I think it's something to do with us fitting so well together.

"So, I am telling you this because I need to be *me* with you. Without that, it's…by far better than what I had with John, yet…it's still not as good as it could be, and I am no longer willing to accept that." The epiphany came to her as she spoke the words, and she suddenly felt conflicted about it. On one hand, it made her feel vulnerable; and on the other, she felt that it was absolutely and imperfectly the only way she was willing to give herself to the man who sat next to her, who loved her for *her*, including her flaws and imperfections.

Patrick was speechless, awaiting her confession, and his anxiety was plain to see. Jasmine wondered if he too was beginning to wonder if they could, in fact, overcome the obstacles placed in their path by fate and their individual pasts.

Apparently unable to handle the suspense any longer, he pleaded with her, "I canna take it anymore, my love. Tell me what it is that ye did, so I can deal with it and move on. I love ye so much, and I canna imagine ye tellin' me anythin' that's like ta make me not love ye, and not want to be close to ye for the rest o' me life. Especially not with everythin' tha's betwixt us."

Jasmine took a deep breath, and then spoke to him in a small and quiet voice, knowing that she was likely to lose him…and along with him, her whole world. "I messed around with Morgan that day, Patrick. That day before I left to get you. And John, he…" She found that she was having difficulty getting the rest of the words out. Finally, mustering as much courage as possible, she sputtered, "John…I let him put his mouth on me while I was pleasuring Morgan."

Now that the admission was complete, Jasmine let out a heavy breath, and unable to look at her beloved as the room grew as quiet as the grave.

Jasmine forced herself to breathe as she tensely awaited his response. Patrick remained motionless and quiet next to her. Finally, she stole a peak at him; when their eyes met, she realized that he had been watching her. Her heart suddenly felt like a small animal was battering its walls, attempting to break loose.

He looked at her expectantly, as if he was waiting for more of her story. Frightened, she didn't know what he needed from her; she had no words left. When the silence stretched uncomfortably, he asked impatiently, "Then what, love? What'd ye do that ye're so worked up about? The suspense is killin' me, woman!"

His voice rose with the last of his demand, and suddenly Jasmine felt an overwhelming urge to laugh. Despite his apparent distress and ire, her hearty laughter broke through, echoing off of the walls. Patrick looked at her as though she had grown three heads, scoffing at her hysterics. Finally, picking himself off of the floor and grabbing the two empty glasses tersely, he walked angrily across the room to refill their wine. All while Jasmine continued to laugh hysterically, tears running down her face.

When she had settled down enough to catch her breath, Patrick demanded, "Now tell me what was so bloody funny, and then finish telln' me what yer confessin' to me, woman!"

Jasmine hiccupped and took a large swallow of wine, fixing him with a merry stare as she said in a joyous voice, "It's what I already told you…about John messing with me."

Processing her words, he stared at her, incredulous, and all but yelled at her, "Ye mean ye was worried about what ye did with yer husband before ye got me back? And what ye was doin' with a lass when it happened, at that?" Jasmine didn't understand his logic, but nodded her head anyway.

Finally seeing the humor of the situation- and no longer fretting over his lover's dark secret- Patrick's mouth curved into a smile before he explained his perspective to her. "I don't see how I coulda been upset with ye, lass, see. John and I already talked about what ye did that day. I reckon it was his way a gettin' me back fer takin' ya from him, but he told me when I first arrived about it.

"He said tha' you didna like when he got to work on touchin' ya, but he kept on all the same, knowin' that if he did it in the right spot while you were occupied with his girl, ye'd be open to it after he got ye all worked up. And he said it made us even, since he did tha' with ye jus' as soon as you and me was getting' together fer good. But don' ye worry yerself about it, love. It was him that did somethin' wrong, not you. I reckon now he and I are even. If we're to live close, and share a family, it's the way it's gotta be. And ye know John…he has to get his revenge."

Jasmine sat quietly for a moment, contemplating his logic, and then asked, "But Patrick, it doesn't bother you that he was with me behind your back?"

Patrick grinned at her and admitted, "Nah! I gave his bollocks a good squeezin' when I learnt, jus' like he did mine."

A giggle escaped Jasmine, quickly cut off by a yawn. Covering it, she remarked on the time, reminding Patrick of his profound need for sleep, as she herded him into the bedroom. When he began to resist her prods, denying his exhaustion, she chided him, saying, "I've never heard you speak so heavily Irish in all your life, Patrick…you need some sleep!"

As she pushed him toward the bedroom, he leaned toward her, nipping her ear as he acquiesced, "Aye, but just because we're heading to the bed, that nay means that we'll be catching some zzzzz's." Winking, he groped her rear playfully.

When they made it to the bed, she shoved him onto his back roughly and demanded that he remove his clothing. Once he obeyed her, she forcibly turned him over. She could see his mind working, trying to figure out which onslaught of sensations she would inflict upon him. What he got completely surprised him, but judging from his expression, it was no less enjoyable. Jasmine doused a warm and oily liquid on his back, her hands working to rub the mixture in.

"Rest, my love, and sleep," she whispered in his ear. He obviously enjoyed her touches, lying still and soaking up the sensation. Within moments, he dozed off, and Jasmine was left with the joy of stroking his well-defined back. She rubbed in circles, kneading, followed by skillful prodding with her fingertips.

His sleep appeared peaceful, marked by his even, relaxed breaths; however, she wanted him to fall into a deep slumber to recover from his recent lack of sleep.

As she massaged, she alternated her ministrations between those given by her hands, and those soothed with her lips. She loved kissing his back and his neck, even when he was asleep. She hoped that her soothing kisses added to the peace of his slumber.

Finally satisfied with her handiwork, she snuggled in next to him, pulling his arm over her. After kissing his neck, she settled in and slept peacefully and blissfully through the night, alongside her beloved.

Patrick awakened, the light of dawn not far off. Slightly disoriented from having slept for so long- and from being in less-than-familiar surroundings- he looked with bleary eyes around the room, remembering all that had recently taken place.

As Jasmine began to stir beside him, a smile lit up his face, and he leaned over her to capture her mouth. Always a light sleeper, Jasmine woke to his affections, returning his kiss. After a moment, inspiration struck him, and he looked down at her and asked, "Would ye come with me for a moment, love? There's something I want to show you."

As she saw the expression on his face, her eyes lit up with excitement, though Patrick had not yet told her where they were going.

He held her robe out to her, fetching her house shoes from the closet before dressing himself. Walking through the sitting area, he grabbed a bottle of wine and two glasses, then held the door open while beckoning her. They entered the courtyard together.

"Just a moment," he told her, handing her the beverage and the goblets. Stepping inside quickly, he pulled the quilt from the couch, wrapping part of it around himself. When he rejoined her, he enclosed her within the warmth as well. They walked together to the patio area, and Patrick sat down, pulling her onto his lap.

"Let me open the wine, love, and then you can pour some for us." She held the bottle toward Patrick as he removed the cork, and she then filled their glasses.

Settling into the haven of quilt and warm body, he kissed her ear, murmuring, "This shall be good, *mo searc*." She sipped while the two sat quietly until the morning sun made its appearance, peeking above the horizon.

The sky brightened, soon alight with glorious hues of pink, orange and gold. Patrick shifted Jasmine on his lap, turning her to face him. Lifting his glass to her, he toasted, and then, with a sigh, he said in a voice that was almost a whisper, quiet but clear, "To us, my love, and to beginning our life with naught between us that would destroy the love and trust we have."

She clinked her goblet against his, and they drank. Draining her glass, she looked to him with tears in her eyes. Reaching gently, he smoothed one tear from her soft cheek, then brought it to his mouth. He knew they were happy tears. Before he could inquire, she said, "No words could've expressed it better, Patrick, and I cherish what we have, just like I'll cherish you for as long as I live."

The couple sat for a time, admiring the colors of the Oklahoma sunrise, enveloped within their shared love, just as they were enclosed in the heat provided by the large comforter. They were aware that there would be challenges ahead- life seemed speckled with them- but for the two of them, there was no one better with whom to face life's obstacles. As each breathed in the other's presence, they both felt that they had found a piece of heaven on earth.

End of Book 2

Preview from Book 3

Maggie awakened in Shannon's arms, naked. When she lifted the blanket she could see that he too, was naked. Noticing the clock across from her, she saw that it was nine p.m. and was surprised to note that they had napped together for several hours.

She looked over at him and studied his features for a moment. His hair was also red, but not quite as bright a hue as hers. He had a thin sprinkling of freckles that ran from cheek to nose to cheek, which she found quite appealing. She could see laugh lines around his mouth and remembered his boisterous chuckle. She thought that he was probably generally good-natured. He had a five o'clock shadow, and she wondered when he had shaved last, or if he was the type that normally went shaggy.

Noticing other areas of his anatomy, she sensed that where their skin touched, there was a sticky feeling, and she thought it was probably from the two of them sweating during their strenuous activities. Though she would typically find that disgusting, reminiscent of the sweaty skin she encountered belonging to her dirty patient's, she found that she didn't mind being sweaty with him. On the contrary, the thought actually turned her on.

Musing over what they had done together, Maggie remembered the feel of him inside of her, and she wanted to see him again. She glanced at him to assure that he was sleeping. Lifting the blanket, she stole a peek. His pubic region was covered by a rich carpet of red curly hairs that corkscrewed over his mons pubis. Just below the area with the thickest covering, his sex organ dominated so that she could scarcely see his scrotum peeking out on either side.

A throaty sound had her turning her head to his face, and she saw that he was watching her with a cocky grin. "Ye like what ye see, do ya" he asked her. She dropped the blanket and laid back, covering her eyes with her hands. She could feel her face burning with embarrassment, and knew that it was bright red. He chuckled at her, bold in his nudity, and then grabbed her at her ribs and teased her, whispering in her ear, "All ye have to do is ask, love, but fair is fair, and I want to look at you too."

His statement caused her to erupt into a volley of giggles, and she turned her head slightly, hiding her face in the pillow. Obviously encouraged, he threw the blanket away from their bodies so that it landed on the floor, and moved to straddle one of her thighs. She resisted, attempting to hold her legs together, but he coaxed her, saying, "Now love, ye got to take a look; I just want the same thing fer meself."

She turned her face away from the pillow and looked at him. "You really want to look at me?" she asked. He smiled down at her, and then assured, "Mmmmm. More than anything, love. And I want to smell ye right here." He said this as he fondled her between her legs, causing her to arch into his fingertips. She was already wet, and he dipped his fingers in and then brought them to his mouth as he made heavy eye contact with her. "Ye taste good, and ye're makin' me mouth water to have ye're flavor on me tongue." As he finished his statement, he brought his mouth to her core and swirled an erotic massage.

As he lapped at her, he drove into her over and over with his fingers so that he stimulated her sensitive nerve endings. Quickly, he had her moaning and writhing; in a thrall from his sensual ministrations. She was frantic from the gathering pleasure he was creating, and he was frenzied from his luscious feeding. Soon, his chin and cheeks were covered in the ambrosia she created.

He was wrapped up in his task, but had to break for air. When he did, he exclaimed through gritted teeth, "Fuck, Maggie, ye're so bloody hot," as he continued to pound into her. When his mouth descended on her again, he swirled his tongue on her nub, quickly increasing the pressure there, and she exploded into his mouth, seeing stars.

The sensations were so intense that she wrapped her thighs around his neck and couldn't help but arch her back off of the couch, remaining affixed to his mouth. He replaced his fingers with his tongue, stabbing the soft tip as deep as it would go, likely in an attempt to extract as much of her sweet flavor as possible.

Finally, he must have had enough, as his ministrations ceased. Shannon gradually released the hold he had on her with his mouth and allowed her to settle onto the couch. Where she was lying against him, Maggie could feel his engorged penis pushing against her leg; she knew that the pressure in his shaft must be overwhelming, as the pleasure he'd just doled out had overwhelmed her. It was confirmed as she gazed up at him, a fevered expression on his face. As her hands roamed his body, he clamped his hands on her hips, in a frenzy to be inside her.

He entered her with a force that pushed her head against the cushy arm of the couch. Though she had just orgasmed, he was building her up again, pistoning into her at the perfect tempo. Each thrust caused bursts of pleasure in exactly the right spot for Maggie, carrying her on a wave of ecstasy until she was pushed over the edge. Gloriously, she orgasmed, gripping his shoulder and pulling him closer to her.

She couldn't see his face; only his neck, but she knew that he was close to the apex as his movements became more frantic. Closing her eyes, she savored the feel of him moving inside her, and yearned for him to reach his climax…she wanted so desperately to return to him the gift that she had just experienced.

Fisting her fingers in his hair in a fit of passion, she held him close to her. Short, grunty sounds escaped his throat as his hips rocked back and forth. Frantically he moved, until finally, with a last vigorous thrust, he exploded into her. The sudden torrent of wetness was unmistakable as his seed spewed into her.

Shannon then collapsed on top of her, the two locked together, unmoving. They remained this way for several moments, spent from their strenuous workout.

About the Author

A. L. LaFleur is a feminist and a professional whose expertise has encompassed areas of forensic nursing that relate to interpersonal violence and violence against women. As such, she has developed a peculiar knowledge of the dynamics and issues involved in those types of situations. Further, having experienced some of the aforementioned circumstances personally, she has chosen to take a stand and speak out against some of the social injustices that continue to plague those of the female gender.

LaFleur lives in a historical neighborhood of Oklahoma City, where she thoroughly enjoys time with friends, family, and the occasional walk to the local bar.

Printed in the United States
By Bookmasters